THE ASYLUM DAUGHTER

ROSIE DARLING

CHAPTER 1

Hushed giggles rippled through the classroom on the top floor of Southwark Workhouse.

"Silence!" barked the matron, slamming her thick hand on the desk.

Beth Thursday jumped. She turned her eyes back to her books and began scribbling furiously. The matron terrified her, with her small dark eyes and cheeks that were a constantly varying shade of red. Her monstrous presence seemed to fill whatever room she entered. Jimmy Wallis's face pulling was funny, to be certain, but Beth was far too scared of the matron to laugh.

The matron had all kinds of punishments for children who misbehaved. Sometimes they were sent to the workhouse kitchens to peel and chop extra vegetables. Sometimes they would go without supper. And sometimes, when children were very bad, the matron would take them from the classroom and march them down the hall to see the workhouse master. The children always came back with tears in their eyes and red welts on their hands and on the backs of their legs.

Beth lived in constant fear of being taken to the workhouse master.

The Southwark workhouse was the only life Beth had ever known. Every morning for eight years she had woken up between its thick stone walls. Every day she crawled out of the bed she shared with three other girls and completed the never-ending list of chores: peeling, chopping, sewing, cleaning. Most days also included the matron's arithmetic lessons. Beth hated those the most.

Beth knew, of course, that there was a world outside the workhouse. From the window of the classroom, she could see over the fence into the street beyond to where carriages trundled down the street and ladies in coloured gowns brought a little brightness to the gloom. It seemed a foreign place. A place she could see but never reach.

Some of the children had memories of the world

outside the workhouse gates. Memories of their lives before their parents had died or left them, or just disappeared. Memories of hunger and cold and sickness and death. Memories of shouting, beatings or men chasing money. Mostly, their stories were not very happy.

Sometimes Beth was glad she had never had to battle the streets of London like some of her friends had. Life in the workhouse was exhausting and the days were long. But it was familiar. She had a bed here, even if she had to share it. She had food here, even if it was flavourless gruel. And never once, in all her eight years, had she ever been lonely.

There was always talk among the children about parents; those mythical creatures who would one day appear to scoop their long-lost offspring from the horrors of the workhouse.

"My papa lives in a big house with lots of servants in it," Jimmy Wallis would say. "And right now he's trying to hunt me down so he can take me back there. I just know it."

"Well, my mama works for the queen," Jane Barrett would exclaim proudly. "In the palace and everything."

Beth, like all the other children, had her own fantasies about who her mother and father were. She kept them to herself, not wanting to be mocked by the other children the way Jane had been. But sometimes at night she lay in bed and tried to picture her mother and father in her mind's eye.

They would be kindly people, of course. And they would have a good reason for having given her up, of course. How they would have hated to do it. How they would have cried. And what joy they would all feel when they were reunited.

They would arrive together at the workhouse and demand to see their daughter. Then they would whisk Beth away from the matron's arithmetic lessons and the endless chores. They would live in a real house and Beth would have a bed all of her own. Perhaps even a *bedroom* all of her own. And they would be a real family.

On the nights that Beth let herself get drawn into this fantasy, she fell asleep with a smile on her face.

But in the morning, the workhouse returned with force. She and the other children would be herded into the dining hall to eat bowls of gruel while the matron's sharp footsteps click-clacked across the stone floor. When her mother and father came to collect her, Beth told herself, she would never again eat another bowl of gruel.

Today, however, that day seemed far away.

Today, Beth could not bring herself to believe her fantasy. Today, she felt certain she would be locked up in the workhouse for the rest of her life.

She looked up at the blackboard at the front of the classroom. Hurriedly scrawled down the sums as she heard the matron's footsteps coming closer.

CHAPTER 2

The workhouse master leant back in his chair and nodded, only half-listening to the demands of the man in front of him.

"She must be an obedient girl," said James Whitaker, pacing back and forth in front of the desk. "Someone agreeable. And intelligent. A fast learner."

The master nodded. Everyone who came here looking to apprentice a child had the same demands. Obedient. Intelligent. Fast learner…

James Whitaker and his wife, the master had learned, were after a young girl to assist them in their tailoring business. The matron had recommended a suitable child.

"Elizabeth Thursday," he told Whitaker. "Eight

years old. A well-behaved child. I believe you will find her most suitable."

Whitaker scratched his bristly chin. "What of her family? Her parents? Any criminal behaviour I ought to know about? Illness, that sort of thing?"

The master opened the register and turned the yellowing pages until he found Elizabeth's entry.

Born in Bethlem Asylum.

He hesitated. If the child had been born in the Bedlam, it meant her mother was unstable at best. The master knew there was a chance the affliction could be passed onto her daughter.

Ought he to say something to Whitaker? No. The girl had already been selected. Her few belongings were being packed. He had no desire to trouble the attendants further. Besides, this Elizabeth had been recommended by the matron. Surely if there was any hint of madness in her character, they would have been noted.

He closed the register. "Nothing of any note, Mr Whitaker. Elizabeth's mother was unable to care for her and gave her up. Like so many of the other poor wretches in this place. Arrived at our door on a Thursday. Hence her name."

Whitaker nodded. "Very well. I should like to meet the girl."

* * *

Beth stood elbow to elbow with the other children, crammed into the workhouse kitchen. As always, there were enormous piles of potatoes to scrub, peel, and chop. More than a hundred souls were now in the workhouse, Beth knew. Men who broke rocks and women who spun yarn. And there was to be enough potatoes peeled and chopped for all of them.

Some days, Beth and the other children spun yarn instead of working in the kitchens. She much preferred this work. Potatoes were simply mashed up and eaten, but the yarn she spun was turned into clothing that would be worn for many years. Beth liked to imagine her yarn being worn by ladies with long, voluminous dresses who attended balls and visited the queen.

But today there was to be no sewing or spinning. Today there was only the never-ending pile of potatoes.

Beth heard footsteps come towards her as she worked away at the peel.

"Miss Thursday?"

Beth swallowed hard at the sound of the matron's voice. She looked up to see the large shadow of the woman looming over her.

"Come with me, please."

Beth's heart thudded. She felt suddenly hot. Why did the matron want to see her? Had she done something wrong? Was she going to come back with red eyes and even redder palms?

She wracked her brain for anything she might have done for which she could be punished. She could think of nothing. She always did her chores quickly and quietly and had finished all her sums yesterday. She had even gotten most of them correct.

She put down her knife, swallowing heavily. Beside her, Jane and Mary Barrett stood with their eyes wide, not daring to say a word.

Nervously, Beth clenched a fist around her skirts and followed the matron towards the office. She could hear Jane and Mary whispering to each other behind her. Beth's mouth grew drier with every step.

The matron led her down a long, gloomy corridor with narrow doors on each side. She had never been in this part of the workhouse before. The thumping of her heart intensified. She was being taken to the workhouse master. She knew it.

Maybe she ought to apologise for whatever it was she had done. Tell the matron how sorry she was for causing trouble. Anything that might prevent her from being punished. Tears of fear welled behind her eyes and she hurriedly blinked them away. She knew the matron hated tears.

But before she could manage a word, the matron rapped sharply on the door before them.

"Come in," a deep voice boomed.

The matron opened the door and ushered Beth inside. The workhouse master, a round-shouldered man with thick grey hair and round glasses, sat behind a desk with a pen in his hand. A second man sat on the opposite side of the table. He was tall and thin, with a long chin and nose. His small, dark eyes fixed on Beth.

She stared nervously up at the two men.

"Elizabeth Thursday, sir," said the matron.

The master nodded. "Thank you." He gave Beth a thin smile. She said nothing, just wrapped her skirts tighter around her fingers.

The man in the chair scratched his pointed chin. "She's very small," he said.

"She's eight years old," said the master, glancing at the records on the table in front of him. "She will grow. Besides, I was under the impression size was unimportant in a business such as yours."

The man hummed noncommittally.

A business such as yours? What were the men

talking about? Beth dared a questioning glance towards the matron, but the woman said nothing.

Finally, the man in the chair nodded. "Very well. She will be satisfactory."

"Very good," said the workhouse master. He scrawled something in his record book, then handed some papers to the tall man. Then he turned to Beth. "You're to go with Mr Whitaker, Miss Thursday," he told her. "You're being apprenticed."

For a moment, Beth said nothing. Apprenticed? She was to leave the workhouse? Venture into the world outside the gates? She was to leave the peeling and chopping and the spinning and the arithmetic? Leave Jane and Jimmy and Mary? She didn't know what to think. Didn't know how to feel. Should she be excited or terrified?

She nodded obediently. She knew it mattered little what she thought or how she felt.

"Yes sir," she squeaked.

Before she could make sense of it, Beth had been pulled out of her white workhouse uniform and told to dress in a thick grey smock. And then she was hurrying out the front door of the workhouse behind Mr Whitaker. Out of the only home she had ever known. She had not even had a chance to say goodbye to her friends.

Mr Whitaker's steps were long and fast, and she had to skip to keep up with him. As they passed through the iron gates, she shot a look back over her shoulder. The brick walls around the workhouse were high and thick and she could see little of the building beyond the top storey and the chimneys that dotted the roof. She had never seen the workhouse from a distance before. Had never appreciated the way the roof sloped so violently, or just how small and dark the windows were.

How strange, thought Beth, that she had spent her life in the place and never truly known what it looked like. And now she was to leave and never return.

Mr Whitaker marched towards a coach waiting on the corner. He clicked open the door. Beth stared for a moment, transfixed by the enormous black wheels of the carriage and the immense height of the dappled grey horse. She had seen horses and carriages through the window many times, of course, but had never imagined they might be so enormous. Mr Whitaker cleared his throat, yanking her from her thoughts. He held out a hand to help her into the coach.

Obediently, Beth scrambled inside and perched on the edge of the bench, her fingers curled around the edge of the seat. Mr Whitaker hauled himself into the carriage and sat opposite her, not speaking. He rapped on the wall of the coach and suddenly they were moving, jolting across the cobbled streets with a rhythmic clatter.

Beth peered out the rain-splattered window. Buildings jostled each other for space on the street and carriages rattled past. Men and women charged up and down the footpaths; some in brightly coloured gowns, others in little more than rags. Newspaper vendors stood on street corners, hollering to passers-by.

Beth let out her breath as they came alongside the wide, dark curve of the river. She had never imagined it to be so vast, so dotted with boats and watermen. She gripped the bench tighter as they clattered over the bridge, the water high and hungry beneath them.

She dared a glance at Mr Whitaker. He had buttoned his coat up to his chin and his long, gloved fingers were folded in his lap. He was looking out the window as though Beth wasn't there. Just the sight of him made her heart race. He was almost as frightening as the matron. Perhaps more so.

But Beth understood. She'd been given a chance at a new life. And she was determined to make the most of it.

CHAPTER 3

*E*mily Whitaker folded the mended jacket carefully and wrapped it in soft brown paper. She handed this to her customer with a smile. "Here you are now. As good as new."

"Exquisite work, Mrs Whitaker," said the woman, clutching the package to her chest. "As always. Thank you ever so much."

Emily smiled. "Of course." She watched the lady disappear from the shop and wave down a passing cab.

As she peered out the window, Emily caught sight of her husband. Her heart skipped a beat. He was marching steadily towards the shop with a young girl at his side. Emily felt a smile spread across her face.

A child brought home from the workhouse. A child in need of love and care. The thought left a warmth in her chest.

All her life she had wanted a child. Prayed for a child. Someone to love and care for, to learn the family business. But she and her husband had never been so lucky.

She stepped out from behind the counter and made her way towards the window, desperate to see more of the girl.

She was small and thin, with long hair in neat plaits down her back. Loose curls danced around her cheeks. Her eyes were wide, and she looked about her as she walked as though she was taking in the city for the very first time.

The poor child looked scared. Emily hoped her husband had been kind to her. She knew it was not companionship James was after. Being childless had not plagued him in the way it had plagued her. He had just shrugged the matter off and labelled it as 'God's will'. But Emily felt a gaping hole within her at not being able to mother a child. It was a hole that could not be filled by the success of her tailoring business, or the love of her husband, or all the luxuries in the world.

For her husband, apprenticing a child from the

workhouse had been no more than a necessity. Their business was growing. They could no longer manage on their own.

James had suggested hiring a seamstress; someone with experience, someone they would not have to bother themselves training. But Emily had had other ideas.

"I always dreamed of passing our business on to our child," she said, her voice wavering slightly. She had just passed her fortieth birthday, and the dream of ever being a mother was growing more and more unattainable. "And I fear it will never be. But I think we ought to find a child to work for us. An apprentice. Teach her everything about the business, just as we would have done with our own child. Someone for whom the business can become her life, just as it is ours."

Someone I can love as a daughter, she thought to herself. But she knew better than to say it.

James sighed hesitantly. "An apprentice?" He shook his head. "We'll have to do far more for this child than just teach her the ways of the business. We'll have to feed her, clothe her, give her a place to sleep."

"There is plenty of room here for a child to

sleep," Emily said, her voice hardening slightly. "And you know it."

For many years, their home above the shop boasted empty rooms and beds that were never slept in. Housing a young apprentice was exactly what this place needed. This house, this business, needed fresh energy, a young person's enthusiasm. It needed a child's voice echoing up and down the halls.

They would find a young apprentice from the workhouse; a child who needed them, just as much as they needed her. Once the idea had entered Emily's mind, she had refused to let go of it. And there was no way she would let her husband convince her otherwise.

It had taken three days of hounding for James to agree to the idea of an apprentice.

"Very well," he had said that morning, letting out a resigned sigh.

Emily shrieked and threw her arms around his neck. "It's the right decision, James, I know it is. You just wait and see." She kissed his bristly cheek, bringing a faint smile to his lips. "You ought to see to it right away. Southwark Workhouse. That's where we'll find our new apprentice."

. . .

THE ASYLUM DAUGHTER

As the two figures drew closer, Emily hurried out the front door to meet them. She beamed down at the girl, who managed a tiny smile in return.

"What's your name, my dear?" she asked gently.

"This is Elizabeth Thursday," James cut in before the girl could open her mouth. "The workhouse master assures me she's a good worker. Well behaved. Intelligent."

Emily smiled at the girl. "I'm sure she is." She put a hand to her shoulder. "Come inside, Elizabeth, my dear. Let me show you your room."

Leaving James in the shop, she led Elizabeth up the narrow staircase that led to their lodgings above. At the top of the staircase, a long corridor stretched through the house with the kitchen and parlour to one side and the two bedrooms on the other.

"You're to make yourself comfortable, my dear," Emily said, as she ushered the girl in and out of each room. "This is your home now and I want you to feel as though you belong."

Elizabeth looked around her as they walked, her dark eyes wide, trying to take it all in. Her gaze roamed over the neat embroidery on the armchairs and the large wooden clock on the mantel.

"My husband and I have lived here ever since we were married," Emily said. "We started our business in the same year." She smiled. "Do you sew, Elizabeth?"

"Yes, ma'am. A little. They taught us at the workhouse."

Emily smiled. "Very good. This afternoon I will show you all the workings in our shop. But first, let's get you settled." She put a gentle hand to the girl's shoulder and was relieved when she didn't flinch. She led her into the bedroom she had set up at the end of the passage.

The girl looked around, wide-eyed. The room was not large but had wide windows that let in streams of afternoon light, even on a grey day like today. The bed in the centre was a decent size. Emily had decorated it with pillows and a blanket embroidered with blue flowers she had made especially for the child. She glanced at Elizabeth. Her lips were parted and her brown eyes shining.

"This is to be your room," Emily told her. "I hope you'll be comfortable here."

The girl looked up at her shyly. "Beth," she said, her voice tiny. "My friends call me Beth."

Emily smiled. "Very well. Beth, it is." She opened the wardrobe to reveal the underskirts and dresses she had stitched in anticipation of their apprentice's arrival. "I've made you some clothes, Beth. Perhaps later you can try them on, and we will alter them if necessary."

She grinned. "Thank you. They're very pretty."

Emily gripped her shoulders and planted a kiss on her forehead. "I'll leave you a moment to get yourself settled, my dear. When you're ready, come out to the kitchen. I'm sure you must be hungry."

Beth stood motionless in the middle of the bedroom, listening to Mrs Whitaker's footsteps retreat down the passage. None of this felt real. How could this room really be hers?

Tentatively, she sat on the bed, feeling the mattress sink invitingly beneath her. Her bed at the workhouse had been almost half the size of this one, and she had shared it with three other girls. She ran her finger over the delicate flowers embroidered on the edge of the blanket. She had never seen anything so beautiful. Had Mrs Whitaker made this, she wondered? Was this the kind of thing Beth was going to learn as an apprentice in their tailoring business? She felt a smile at the corners of her lips.

She went to the wardrobe and peered at the four dresses hanging on the rail. They were all made of fine wool: one pale green, one floral and two in different shades of blue. Clothes made just for her. Beth could hardly believe it.

Her stomach groaned loudly, reminding her she had been taken from the workhouse before their afternoon meal.

She made her way towards the doorway and then stopped. She could hear Mr and Mrs Whitaker's voices drifting up from the shop downstairs. Beth crept to the top of the stairs and listened.

"Where is the girl?" Mr Whitaker asked tersely.

"In her room getting settled."

"What is she doing in there? We didn't bring her here so she could lounge around the house all day. She's got things to learn."

"Oh James," Mrs Whitaker huffed, "give the poor girl a little time to find her feet. This must all be very new to her. I'll see her settled and fed and then I'll bring her down to the shop."

Beth felt the muscles in her neck tense. She hated the thought of Mr and Mrs Whitaker arguing because of her. She hurried away from the stairs as the door at the bottom clicked open. Mrs Whitaker climbed the stairs back up to the living quarters.

Her smile was wide and warm as though she had not just been arguing with her husband. "Come, my dear," she said, ushering Beth into the kitchen. "I made some soup and fresh bread this morning. I'm sure you must be hungry."

THE MOMENT BETH finished her soup, Mr Whitaker appeared beside the table. Had he been watching her from the hallway, Beth wondered? Had he pounced on her the second he had seen her lift the last spoonful to her lips?

"Come on, child. This way." His voice was firm. Beth stood abruptly and followed him down the stairs and into the shop, managing a hurried thanks to Mrs Whitaker.

"We are one of the most highly-regarded tailors in west London," Mr Whitaker said, pride swelling his voice. He looked pointedly at Beth. "And we intend to keep it that way."

"Of course, sir," she squeaked. Her heart was thundering.

"My wife and I will see to it that you are properly trained in all areas of the business," he said. "Serving customers, handling accounts and payments, and of course, tailoring itself. In return, you will ensure your work is of the highest calibre. We will not accept sloppy workmanship or laziness. Do I make myself clear?"

"Yes sir," Beth managed.

"Good." Mr Whitaker marched into a small room at the back of the shop, making Beth skip to catch up with him.

Shelves ran along one wall, laden with fabrics in a multitude of colours. Beth felt an involuntary smile creep across her face. At the workhouse, she had only ever sewed with plain white linen and spun colourless yarn. She couldn't wait to stitch with such beautiful fabrics.

"Linen and muslin," Mr Whitaker told her, gesturing to the shelves. "Wool and cotton. And over here, silk and satin. We have clients from all classes of society, Miss Thursday. And for each of them, we produce work of the highest quality. We take no shortcuts here, am I understood?"

Beth nodded obediently, transfixed by the rainbow of fabrics. "Yes, sir. Of course."

She knew she was good at needlework. Her stitching was neat and tiny, her measurements accurate. Even the stony-faced matron had once complimented her work.

So when Mr Whitaker said: "You have basic needlework skills, I hope?"

Beth nodded and said, "Yes sir, I do," in the clearest voice she had managed all day.

Mr Whitaker led her to the sewing table in the corner of the storeroom. The beginnings of what Beth assumed to be a woman's shift were laid out on the table. Mr Whitaker nodded towards it. "This piece needs hemming. Show me what you can do."

Beth sat at the table and threaded the needle. As she picked up the shift, she realised it was soft cotton, not the coarser linen she was used to. A frown of concentration creasing the bridge of her nose, and she began to sew, quickly but carefully, creating a row of tiny stitches along the hem of the shift.

She held the finished product out to Mr Whitaker. He took it from her hands, examining it closely. Beth could tell he was trying hard to find a flaw.

Finally, he nodded and held it out to her. "It's good work," he said stiffly.

Beth was unable to hold back a smile.

THAT NIGHT she collapsed into her enormous bed, pulling the blanket to her chin. She stretched out her arms and legs, revelling in the fact that there was no one beside her.

She was exhausted, both physically and mentally. She had spent the afternoon learning about all the different types of fabrics in the storeroom, then she had swept the shop floor and polished the windows. By the time she had sat down to supper, her legs were aching, and her eyes were heavy. But as she lay back in her palatial bed, a broad smile was etched on her face. Despite Mr Whitaker's firm hand, Beth knew she was extraordinarily lucky to have been brought here. She had a chance to make something of herself. Make something of her life. And she was not going to waste such an opportunity.

CHAPTER 4

Cooking with Mrs Whitaker, Beth quickly came to realise, was a very different experience to working in the kitchen at the workhouse. Peeling and chopping vegetables was far less nerve-wracking without the clip-clop of the matron's footsteps in the background.

Still, Beth found herself wondering why she had been so afraid of the matron. When the old woman had appeared to take her to master's office, she had been whisked away from the workhouse to a home with a bed of her own and the loving Mrs Whitaker.

Each night after the shop closed, Beth would join Mrs Whitaker in the kitchen, learning to make bread and cakes and countless other dishes she had never heard of.

She discovered that she loved jam. Discovered porridge was not complete without a healthy dose of treacle. And she discovered that the smell of roasting meat was simply heavenly after a long day's work.

Beth stood close to the oven, inhaling deeply as the rich aroma filled the kitchen. "It smells so good," she gushed. "I wish we could eat it right now!"

Mrs Whitaker chuckled. "I assure you, my dear, it will taste far better if we wait a little longer." She ran a gentle hand over Beth's dark hair and smoothed the stray strands behind her ears. "It's nice to have someone who appreciates my cooking," she said with a smile. "I sometimes think my James would eat gutter slops and not blink an eye."

Beth giggled. "We hardly ever ate meat in the workhouse," she told Mrs Whitaker matter-of-factly.

"No? What did you eat instead?"

Beth smiled. She liked it when Mrs Whitaker asked her questions. Mr Whitaker rarely spoke to her outside of giving instructions, and when he did, he never mentioned the workhouse. Beth wasn't sure why. After all, it was hardly a secret as to where she had come from. Mr Whitaker had scooped her from the place himself. It was almost as though he was ashamed of the fact that he had a workhouse orphan residing under his roof.

But Beth was not ashamed of her past. She liked it when Mrs Whitaker showed an interest in her previous life up to the time of their involvement.

"We ate porridge mostly," Beth told her. "And potatoes. We had to peel them all ourselves. There always seemed to be so many of them. And we never ate roast beef. Or treacle."

"You're a hard worker, aren't you, Beth?" Mrs Whitaker said kindly. "We were ever so lucky to find you."

Beth lowered her eyes, her cheeks colouring. She knew she was the lucky one. Sometimes, when she crawled into her enormous feather bed each night, she found herself thinking of Jimmy and Jane and Mary and all the other children at the workhouse. She hoped they too had found themselves apprenticeships. She hoped they were eating treacle on their porridge too. But deep within herself, Beth knew it was unlikely.

"Have you brothers and sister and the like?" she asked Mrs Whitaker suddenly. There was so much she longed to know about the woman who had become something of a mother to her. With each question Mrs Whitaker asked her, Beth felt more and more comfortable asking questions of her own.

"Oh yes," said Mrs Whitaker, smiling broadly.

"I've two sisters and two brothers. I was the baby of the family. They all spoilt me rotten. In my dear papa's eyes, I could never do a thing wrong. Used to drive my mother mad."

Beth giggled. She tried to imagine Mrs Whitaker as a young child. It was something of a challenge, she realised. Mrs Whitaker seemed oddly ageless, as though she would never grow older and had never been younger.

Mrs Whitaker reached out and stroked Beth's messy hair. "Perhaps we might visit them one day. It would make me ever so happy for them to meet you." She sighed, a warm smile on her face. "I would just love for them to see how happy you have made me."

* * *

"Time for bed, Beth," said Emily, once they had finished the meal.

Beth nodded obediently and stood up from her chair.

"Clear the plates first," barked James. Emily felt anger prickle the back of her neck. She hated the way her husband spoke to the girl sometimes.

Beth gathered the plates without speaking and

carried them into the kitchen. Emily could hear the sloshing of the water as she placed them in the trough. She got to her feet and hurried into the kitchen.

"There's no need to wash those, my dear," she told Beth from the doorway. "You go off to bed and I'll see to the dishes."

Beth peered over her shoulder. "Are you certain?"

"Of course," said Emily. "You need your sleep. Quick now. Bedtime." She planted a kiss on the top of Beth's head and pulled her into her arms. "Sleep well, my dear."

The girl smiled, then pattered down the hall in her stockinged feet. Emily felt a smile at the corner of her lips as she watched Beth disappear.

She had spent so many years longing to hear a child's footsteps running up and down her hall. Beth was not her own child, of course, but that didn't stop the great swell of love Emily had begun to feel for the girl. She had always longed to be a mother. And a mother was exactly what little Beth Thursday needed.

She turned back to the dishes, sighing happily. Heavy footsteps behind her alerted her to her husband's presence.

"Emily," James said tersely. "This has to stop." He

slid his hand around the top of her arm, turning her to face him.

She tried to shake her arm free, but his grip tightened. "*What* has to stop?"

James sighed, releasing her. "Treating the girl like she's our daughter. Giving her goodnight kisses and doing her chores for her. Speaking of your family to her. She's not our child. She's our *worker*. And it would do you well to remember it." He folded his arms, a frown darkening his narrow face. "It would do you both well."

Emily glared, planting a hand on her hip. "What do you mean by that?"

"The girl is getting lazy," said James. "She shouldn't have had to be told to clear the dishes. And she knows you'll never scold her for it."

"Lazy!" Emily cried. "Beth is the hardest worker I've ever seen! And her sewing is excellent. You know that."

James snorted. "If you continue treating her like this, it will only be a matter of time before the calibre of her work begins to suffer." He opened the door of the range to check the fire, then slammed it again with far more force than was necessary. "And she is not to visit your family, do you hear me? It would be most inappropriate!"

Emily sighed. She pressed her hands to her husband's shoulders and looked him in the eye. James Whitaker was a hard, strait-laced man, Emily knew well, but she also knew there was decency in him. There was kindness there if only you looked hard enough.

"Please James," she said gently. "Show a little humanity. A little kindness. We're the only family the poor girl has ever known."

She looked into his eyes, imploring.

"No," James said sharply. "We are not. The girl is an orphan. She has no family. She is our apprentice. Nothing more."

BETH CURLED UP IN A BALL, pulling her blanket over her head to block out Mr Whitaker's fierce voice. Despite herself, his words had made tears prick her eyes.

An orphan. Was that really what she was? How desperately she wanted to believe her mother was out there somewhere.

She was endlessly grateful for Mrs Whitaker's kindness, but Mr Whitaker's outbursts reminded her that she would never truly belong here. She would never really have a family of her own.

She has no family. She is our apprentice, nothing more.

Beth pressed her hands to her ears, trying to stop the words from circling through her mind. He was right. She was an orphan from the workhouse. And that was all she would ever be.

CHAPTER 5

Four years had passed since Mr Whitaker had scooped Beth from the workhouse. She spent long days serving customers and mending and hemming clothes, and she had even started to make simple gowns on her own. The days were long and tiring, but Beth relished each minute. She had come to know almost all their customers by name and enjoyed chatting with them and hearing about their lives.

While Mr Whitaker remained strict and professional, he had come to appreciate Beth's skill with a needle and thread. Had come to realise many of his customers returned just to chat with his friendly young apprentice. The tension between them – and between Mr and Mrs Whitaker – had largely faded away.

Nonetheless, Beth's favourite times were the evenings in which Mr Whitaker went off to the tavern, leaving her and Mrs Whitaker alone.

When their workload was full, as it often was, they would spend the evenings sewing in front of the fire, chatting amicably to each other. Other times, Mrs Whitaker would teach her new skills around the house, the art of jam making, or to embroider delicate designs, like the one on the edge of Beth's blanket.

Mrs Whitaker was the closest thing to a mother Beth had ever known. But as much as she loved the woman, Beth was unable to still the restlessness inside her. Unable to stop wondering about where she had truly come from.

"Is it true that I'm an orphan?" she asked Mrs Whitaker one evening as they sat together in the parlour mending clothing.

Mrs Whitaker lowered the dress she was holding. There was a hint of surprise on her face. In the four years Beth had been working for the Whitakers, it was the first time she had spoken aloud of her parents.

For a moment, she worried that she might have

upset Mrs Whitaker. The last thing she wanted was to seem ungrateful. Mrs Whitaker had made her life immeasurably better. But all the love in the world had not been enough to silence Beth's internal questions.

She was relieved when a small smile appeared on Mrs Whitaker's face. Her blue eyes were filled with understanding.

"Oh Beth," she said gently, "I wish I had an answer for you. I know how difficult it must be to not know these things. But I'm afraid I just don't know. The workhouse master didn't have that information, and so neither do we."

Beth nodded, trying not to let the disappointment get to her. She had known it unlikely that Mrs Whitaker would have the answers she so desperately sought. After all, if she had known something about Beth's mother, surely she would have said something earlier.

Mrs Whitaker reached out of the armchair and smoothed Beth's unruly dark curls. "I'm sorry, my dear. Perhaps you may have to make peace with the fact that you will never know."

Beth nodded, her throat tight. "Yes. Perhaps. It's all right. Truly. I just thought that maybe…" she faded out hopelessly.

Mrs Whitaker gave her an understanding smile. "We all want to know who we are," she said. "Where we come from." She took Beth's cheeks in her hands, the way she had done when Beth was younger. "You are your own person, Beth. And a fine person at that. Who your parents were, where they came from, it doesn't change that."

Beth nodded, blinking away her tears.

Mrs Whitaker yawned, rubbing her eyes and folding the dress over the arm of the chair. "I'm exhausted, my love. I'm afraid I'm going to have to finish that in the morning."

Beth chewed her lip. Mrs Whitaker was always tired lately. Not that Beth could blame her. Most days, they worked in the shop from dawn until long after the sun had set. And then there was the cooking and the cleaning to do; cooking and cleaning that, despite Beth's protests, Mrs Whitaker insisted on largely handling herself. Beth wished she would rest a little more. Though Mrs Whitaker was far from old, she knew no one could keep up such a workload forever.

"I can finish it for you," she said. "Once I've done mine."

"Oh no," said Mrs Whitaker. "There's no need to do that."

Beth smiled. "It's no bother. I'd be happy to do it."

Mrs Whitaker planted a kiss on Beth's forehead. "You are a wonder, my dear. I don't know how we ever got by without you."

Beth smiled to herself as she watched Mrs Whitaker disappear down the passage to her bedroom. Perhaps she would never know where she had come from. Perhaps she would never know who she really was. But she had Mrs Whitaker. She had a roof over her head, and she had a job she loved. Perhaps that was all she needed.

CHAPTER 6

Two days later, Beth padded out to the kitchen to find it uncharacteristically empty. Where was Mrs Whitaker? Every morning for the four years she had been here, Beth had come to the kitchen to find a fire crackling in the range and the kettle steaming. Mrs Whitaker would be kneading bread dough or stirring porridge, her face lighting as Beth appeared in the doorway.

Her absence gave Beth an uncomfortable shiver.

Surely there was nothing wrong, she told herself. Mrs Whitaker had been working far too hard lately. No doubt she was just having a much-needed rest.

Beth set to work lighting the fire. She sat the kettle on the range and took the jar of oats from the shelf, pouring some into a pot for porridge.

As she stirred the contents, she listened carefully for any sounds from Mr and Mrs Whitaker's bedroom. Nothing. The knot in her stomach tightened.

Beth tried to push it away.

Everything is all right, she told herself again. *Mrs Whitaker is just resting.* And Mr Whitaker was likely fast asleep beside her.

As Beth was spooning the porridge into three bowls, she heard the thunder of footsteps on the stairs. Mr Whitaker came charging into the house, trailed by a man in a long black coat.

Beth dropped the serving spoon, letting it clatter noisily against the rim of the pan.

"Mr Whitaker?"

He and the man in black charged into Mrs Whitaker's bedroom, not giving Beth so much as a glance.

Abandoning the porridge, Beth hurried down the hall and pressed her ear to the door of the bedroom. She could hear mumbled voices but couldn't make out their words. Was he a physician, she wondered? Was Mrs Whitaker unwell?

Beth shivered, wrapping her arms around herself.

She hovered outside the room for a few

moments, unsure of what to do. She had best open the shop, she decided. After all, what was she but Mr and Mrs Whitaker's apprentice? It was what was expected of her.

Her appetite gone, Beth threw the untouched porridge into the bin and made her way down to the shop. She went to the back room and found the shift she was hemming, bringing it out into the shop so she could continue working on it from behind the counter.

After what felt like an eternity, the man in black made his way downstairs, followed by Mr Whitaker. The two men spoke to each other in mumbled voices.

"What's happening?" Beth demanded once the man in black had left. "Was he a physician? Is Mrs Whitaker unwell?"

Mr Whitaker wrapped his arms around himself. "Just do your work, Elizabeth," he said stiffly. He didn't look her in the eyes. Impulsively, she grabbed his arm as he made his way back towards the staircase.

"Please, sir. Tell me what's happening. I need to know." Her eyes met his imploringly.

"The physician is doing all he can," he said stiffly.

Beth felt a sudden wave of fear wash over her.

"What is it?" she asked, her voice coming out husky. "What does she have?"

Mr Whitaker drew in his breath. "The physician believes it to be cholera."

Beth felt tears prick her eyes. She had seen cholera sweep through the workhouse back when she was a child. Had watched it take lives in days, sometimes less.

A stray tear slipped down her cheek and she pushed it away hurriedly. She opened her mouth to speak but could find no words. A stilted silence hung between them.

"Get back to work," Mr Whitaker said finally. "We have a business to run."

THE DAY PASSED in a blur with Beth unable to think of anything but Mrs Whitaker lying ill in her bed. She knew there was every chance she would not last through the night. The thought brought an ache to her chest more violent than anything she had ever experienced. How could she lose Mrs Whitaker? How would she go on?

Beth locked the front door of the shop and made her way upstairs. Her stomach was rolling, and her eyes stung from the tears that had plagued her throughout the day.

The rooms upstairs were silent, apart from the muffled groans that came from behind Mrs Whitaker's bedroom door.

Beth went to the kitchen, not knowing what else to do. She had not eaten all day, but she had not even a scrap of an appetite.

Tea, she decided. Tea had always been able to calm her. Had always made things feel a little more manageable.

She set the kettle on the range and stared at it until it began to boil. She poured herself a cup and brought it slowly to her lips. It slid warm down her throat but did little to calm her. Instead, it brought a fresh rush of tears.

Beth set her cup down on the edge of the table. She needed to see Mrs Whitaker. What did it matter if she got sick herself?

She went to the bedroom and knocked on the door.

"What do you want?" Mr Whitaker's voice was thin.

"Please may I come in?"

Beth heard footsteps crossing the room. Mr Whitaker opened the door and peered out at her.

"You're not to enter, do you understand? You could very well get sick yourself. And where would the business be then?"

"Please," Beth coughed. "I just need to see her." She tried to peer past him into the room, but he blocked her way.

"Elizabeth," he said. "Please." She had never heard such emotion in his voice before. In the pale light of the hall lamp, Beth could see his eyes were red-rimmed. It made her stomach lurch.

"I want to see my mother," she heard herself say. The words surprised her. It was true, she realised, Mrs Whitaker *had* become her mother. She watched the same surprise pass over Mr Whitaker's face.

"She is not your mother!" he hissed, his bristly face close to hers. "She is not!"

Tears spilt suddenly down Beth's cheeks. "Is she going to die?"

Mr Whitaker said nothing. His clenched his jaw so tightly that it shook. "Get out of here, Elizabeth," he said finally. "Stay and you'll likely get sick too."

Beth went back to the kitchen. She carried her cup downstairs and made her way into the storeroom.

. . .

She did not make it to bed until long after midnight. All night, she stayed downstairs in the shop, sewing by lamplight, desperate to keep herself busy. Stop work and the reality of the situation would come charging back. Mrs Whitaker was dying. Beth knew there was no point in pretending otherwise.

Finally, unable to keep her eyes from drooping, she packed away the dress she was hemming and carried her lamp upstairs.

She pressed an ear to the door of Mr Whitaker's bedroom. She could hear him breathing deeply and rhythmically. She continued down the hall until she reached Mrs Whitaker's room. She opened the door a crack and peeked inside. Mrs Whitaker lay on her back, her face lit by a shaft of moonlight peeking through the curtains.

She looked small and frail, the lines in her cheeks and forehead much more pronounced than Beth remembered. The room smelled sour, like sickness and death.

Beth didn't care. She needed to be close to her. Right now, more than ever, she needed to be with the woman who had cared for her when no one else had. The woman who had been the closest thing to a mother Beth had ever known.

She slid the chair from the corner of the room to the side of Mrs Whitaker's bed. She perched on the edge and held the woman's hand in both of hers. Her fingers felt skeletal and cold. The feel of them brought a violent pain to Beth's throat.

Mrs Whitaker opened her eyes. She turned her head on the pillow.

"Beth," she rasped, "what are you doing in here? You mustn't—"

Tears spilt down Beth's cheeks. "I had to see you," she coughed.

Mrs Whitaker gave Beth's hand a feeble squeeze. "It's all right, my darling," she said huskily. "Everything is going to be all right."

Beth's tears fell harder. "It's not all right!" she cried. "I know it's not!" She wiped her eyes, shuffling onto the bed and curling up beside Mrs Whitaker. "I don't want to lose you."

Mrs Whitaker pushed gently against her shoulder, making her sit. "You are going to be just fine without me, Beth," she said, attempting a smile. "You're a strong and brave young lady with your whole life ahead of her. You can get through anything."

Beth wiped her eyes, shaking her head violently. "No."

She didn't feel strong. All she wanted to do was crumple into a heap and sob until her throat was raw.

"You've a talent with a needle and thread, and you have a talent with people. Those things are going to get you far in life. I've never been more sure of anything." Mrs Whitaker gave another feeble smile. "Now please, my love. You must leave. I couldn't bear it if you got sick too."

Beth gave Mrs Whitaker's hand a final squeeze and stood up from the chair, her heart aching. She knew it would be the last time she would ever see her adoptive mother alive. The thought made a sob well up from deep inside her. She covered her mouth to keep it inside. Mrs Whitaker believed she was strong. And Beth was determined not to disappoint her.

The moment she was out of the bedroom, she raced down the hallway and into her own room. Beth threw herself into bed and pulled the covers up over her head. She pressed her face into her pillow to muffle her sobs. How was she to go on without Mrs Whitaker? Now she had experienced what it was like to be loved, how was she to go on without it?

CHAPTER 7

Three days later, Beth stood in the graveyard at Saint Stephen's and watched as Mrs Whitaker's coffin was lowered into the earth. The churchyard was crowded with mourners, many of whom Beth recognised as customers.

The first snow of the season had fallen the night before, dusting the earth in white. Beth wrapped her arms around herself and shivered, the cold wind stinging the tip of her nose. She let her tears fall freely

Mr Whitaker stood on the other side of the grave, his dark coat buttoned to his chin and his head bent. His top hat was pulled down low, the brim almost obscuring his eyes.

Beth felt an ache in her chest as she watched him. His jaw was clenched tightly as though to ward off any public display of emotion, but Beth could see the grief simmering beneath the surface. A part of her longed to throw her arms around him in comfort. Another part of her was terrified of the man, and the life alone with him that lay before her. Mrs Whitaker had always been the one to keep the peace between them. She had soothed her husband's tempers, had coaxed out the occasional smile. Beth could barely begin to imagine how she would manage without her.

Neither spoke in the cab home. Mr Whitaker sat with his gaze fixed on the ice-streaked window, his long fingers knotted together. Beth perched on the bench seat opposite him, playing with the buttons on her coat. She could tell this stilted silence was one that would pervade their home now.

The coach slowed as it reached the shop and they climbed out without speaking. Beth followed Mr Whitaker inside, their footsteps echoing through the emptiness. The house had never felt so cold and unwelcoming.

Beth hovered at the bottom of the stairwell, unsure what to do. "Perhaps I might make us some supper?" she ventured, her voice stuck in her throat.

Mr Whitaker shook his head. "I'm not hungry. And there's work to do. We've already fallen far behind with all that's happened."

Beth swallowed heavily. She understood. She too was reluctant to go up to their lodgings and exist in the place without Mrs Whitaker. How could they bear such a thing?

Perhaps working was the best thing for them. There would be no need for them to speak, and it would go some way to preventing them from dwelling on all they had lost.

She made her way silently into the back room and slipped into her chair at the sewing table. Behind her, she could hear the *scratch scratch* of Mr Whitaker's pen as he churned through the accounts.

It was long past midnight when the scratching of the pen fell silent. Beth looked over her shoulder. Mr Whitaker had fallen asleep in his chair, his head drooped, and ink splattered down the front of his shirt and waistcoat.

Beth put down her sewing. She needed to sleep too. Needed to eat. She had put off going upstairs for long enough.

Drawing in her breath, she tiptoed up to the lodgings. The lamp in her hand cast long shadows across the silent rooms. Beth felt an ache in her chest. How many times had she climbed upstairs from the shop to help Mrs Whitaker cook supper? How many times had they sat in front of the fire in the parlour, talking about everything and nothing?

She wiped a stray tear away with the back of her hand. Beth stepped into the dark kitchen and broke the end off of a loaf of stale bread. She popped it into her mouth to quiet her groaning stomach, then she slipped into bed and fell into an exhausted sleep.

WITHOUT MRS WHITAKER, it felt as though the house's heart had stopped beating. Beth did her best to keep the routine running as it had before; ensuring meals were on the table, keeping up with orders and managing the customers. But she did all of it with a heaviness in her heart she was afraid would never ease.

She found it hard to look at Mr Whitaker. In his eyes, she could see the same deep ache that had taken root inside her. Sometimes, for fleeting seconds, Beth considered talking to him about all they had lost. Perhaps sharing a little of their grief might make it easier to carry. But each time she was about to open her mouth, Mr Whitaker would fix her with his steely eyes and Beth would be reminded that, as far as he was concerned, she was nothing but his employee.

When they were working in the shop together, Mr Whitaker spoke to Beth as little as possible; communicating in single words or abrupt, emotionless sentences. Around the house, they were wordless. Breakfasts were spent peering into porridge bowls, and after silent suppers, Beth would go straight to bed.

It wasn't long before Mr Whitaker took to drink.

At first, he just disappeared from the house more often than before. Beth assumed he was making his regular visits to the tavern. But soon he resorted to simply collapsing in the sitting room with a bottle in his hand. Beth awoke on many mornings to find him dozing in the same chair he had been sitting in when she had gone to bed the night before, a half-drunk bottle lying at his feet.

Soon, the business began to suffer. Bleary-eyed with whisky, Mr Whitaker's accounting became sloppy and inaccurate. On many occasions, Beth found herself huddled beside a candle in her bedroom, rewriting Mr Whitaker's invoices until long after midnight.

Soon enough, he stopped working at all.

. . .

WITH THE WEIGHT of the entire business on her shoulders, Beth did her best to keep the shop afloat. She awoke before dawn each morning to work on the dressmaking orders, then hurried back upstairs to prepare breakfast. While the shop was open, she would alternate between working in the backroom and darting out to the front when she heard the bell above the door announce a customer's arrival. She spent most nights doing the accounts at the supper table while her eyelids drooped, and her legs ached. She would stumble to bed close to midnight before waking several hours later and doing it all again.

Though she was constantly tired, her mind refused to stop churning. She knew well that Mr Whitaker had taken to gambling; frittering away their meagre profits at the whist tables. How long would she be able to keep the shop open on her own? Would Mr Whitaker's health continue to deteriorate? And what would happen to her if he died? Would she be sent back to the workhouse?

And there, behind all the worries, was that nagging question that refused to leave her.

Who is my real mother?

The need to know had intensified after Mrs

Whitaker's death. In her four years of being cared for and loved by her adoptive mother, Beth had largely been able to push the question to the back of her mind. She knew how lucky she was to have been taken from the workhouse by a woman who had loved her. Pining after her birth mother – the woman who had given her up – felt wrong.

But with Mrs Whitaker gone, Beth felt achingly alone. Even in her worst days at the workhouse, she had been surrounded by the other boys and girls. Her friends had cared about her, even if the master and matron had not.

But now? What did Mr Whitaker care if something was to happen to her? She felt certain he would only notice she was gone when his supper failed to appear.

In Mrs Whitaker's care, Beth had had a taste of what it was like to be loved. And how desperately she craved it.

But she was no longer the naïve young child she had been in the workhouse. In a few months, she would be thirteen. And as she approached her teen years, she could feel her old fantasies falling away, replaced by the chill of reality.

How many children from the workhouse were

ever reunited with their parents? Beth did not know of a single one.

No, she knew it was near impossible that she would ever discover the truth about who she was. Even more impossible that she would be reunited with her parents. In all likelihood, her mother had sold her body on the streets. And it was also more than likely that she had not loved her baby daughter. Even if her mother was by miracle still alive, what chance was there she would want her child back?

Reality, Beth decided, was cold and cruel. How she wished she could disappear into her fantasy world the way she had when she was a little girl. How she wished she could let herself believe, even for a second, that someone was coming to save her.

CHAPTER 8

Despite the bitter intrusion of reality, Beth was unable to silence that voice inside her that was asking questions about her mother. It wasn't about finding someone to love her, she realised – she had become too wise for that. No, it was about understanding who she was and how she had ended up where she had.

One evening after supper, Beth found herself hovering in the doorway of the parlour. Mr Whitaker had returned home from the tavern an hour ago and was now half asleep in the armchair. His head was lolling to one side, one long arm draped over the edge of the chair, fingers grazing the half-drunk bottle on the floor beside him.

Beth stared at him. Was it possible, she

wondered, that he might have some information about her birth mother? After all, he had been the one to collect her from the workhouse. Mrs Whitaker had told her they had been given no information, but perhaps Mr Whitaker had simply never told his wife what he knew. Perhaps he had thought it of no consequence. After all, what was she to him but their apprentice?

She knotted her fingers together. She had to ask.

"Mr Whitaker?"

He opened an eye slowly and peered at her. Just as Beth decided he was not going to speak, he barked, "What it is?"

She swallowed hard, her nerves jangling. She had shared a home with this man for more than four years. How was it that she was still so terrified of him?

"I just…" she faded out, the words caught in her throat.

Mr Whitaker sat up. "You what, girl? Spit it out."

Beth sucked in her breath. "I wanted to ask you about my mother." She swallowed. "My birth mother."

Mr Whitaker hauled himself out of his chair, knocking over the bottle in the process and cursed loudly. He stood over Beth, peering down at her with cold, dark eyes. Beth could smell whisky and tobacco on his breath. An untidy grey beard had sprouted on his cheeks and chin. "Your birth mother?" he repeated slowly.

Beth nodded. "Yes. I just thought... Do you know who she is?"

She reeled backwards at an unexpected flash of pain to her cheek. It took a moment to realise Mr Whitaker had struck her. Instinctively, she pressed a hand to her face. Tears of shock welled in her eyes and she hurriedly blinked them away.

"Ungrateful wretch," he spat. "My wife gave you everything and you repay her by asking after your birth mother? You know she loved you like her own child. You were everything to her." His voice wavered.

Beth swallowed the violent pain in her throat. "I'm so sorry. I didn't mean... I loved Mrs Whitaker too," she coughed. "Truly. I loved her more than anyone."

Mr Whitaker snorted. "Your birth mother is dead," he spat. "You killed her, just like you killed my wife."

Beth felt suddenly cold. "What?" she managed. Her thoughts knocked together as she tried to piece together Mr Whitaker's accusations. Did he truly hold her responsible for his wife's death? And was he telling the truth about her birth mother? Or was he just saying such things to punish her?

"That's right," he hissed. "My Emily would still be alive if you hadn't worn her into the ground with your laziness. She spent every minute of every day working and caring for you. Doing the chores that ought to have been yours." He jabbed a bony finger under her nose. "It's your fault she's gone, girl. And I will never forgive you."

The tears Beth had been fighting slipped suddenly down her cheeks. She turned abruptly and raced out of the room.

CHAPTER 9

*B*eth stood over the range, stirring the watery soup. Today there was even less meat in the pot than there had been last time. Soon she'd be making broth with nothing but animal bones.

Beth sighed heavily and spooned the soup into a bowl. With luck, Mr Whitaker would be too drunk to notice how pitiful the soup had become.

It had been five years since Mrs Whitaker's death, and each of those five years had seen her husband descend further into a life of gambling and drunkenness. Beth couldn't remember the last time she had seen him sober.

Somehow, miraculously, Beth had managed to keep the shop afloat, though the profits disappeared at the gambling houses before she could even count them. All she knew was the soup was getting more and more watery and their coal baskets were constantly empty. She could hardly remember the last time she had not been hungry. Could hardly remember when last she had not been cold.

But, she reasoned as she carried the soup into the parlour for Mr Whitaker, she had a roof over her head and a bed of her own. And that had to count for something.

Mr Whitaker was asleep in the armchair. When he was not at the taverns or the gambling houses, he spent most of his time here, with his head lolling and an arm dangling above the floor.

She set the bowl on the small table beside the chair. "Your lunch, Mr Whitaker," she said, not expecting a response.

He grunted, not opening his eyes. As Beth turned to leave, he mumbled, "Light the fire."

"There's not enough coal," Beth told him.

He snorted. "I'm cold, girl," he said bitterly. "I told you to light the fire."

Beth felt the anger bubble under her skin. "There's no coal," she said again, more firmly. "If I light the fire for you now, we'll have no way of cooking for the rest of the week."

Mr Whitaker cursed under his breath, but gave up, his eyes falling closed again.

Beth pulled the door closed firmly and marched down to the shop.

These days, customers were few and far between. Beth knew her workload and constant exhaustion were having a negative effect on her handiwork. And then there was the fact that they could no longer afford the beautiful silks and satins they had once used to fashion the gowns. The rainbow of colours inside the storeroom had diminished to a bland stack of colourless linen. These days, most of her work came from simple repairs that paid little. Beth didn't blame the regular customers who had gradually begun to slip away.

She took her seat at the sewing table and began to work at replacing a row of buttons on a man's smoking jacket. The task was simple and uninspiring. How she longed to create gowns from silk and satin again. How she longed to design and embroider and see ladies' faces light up when they saw her creations. Still, she told herself, she ought to be happy with whatever work she could get. She was sure it wouldn't be long before there were no more buttons to replace at all.

The bell above the door jangled loudly and Beth

climbed to her feet, making a silent wish for a new customer. She plastered on her most genial smile.

A well-dressed woman was gliding into the shop, her dark blue woollen gown sighing across the floorboard. Her feathered hat was perched on top of a pile of dark curls. Beth's heart began to quicken. This woman had money – and lots of it. Secure a sale here and she and Mr Whitaker would have enough to keep the fires burning for as long as they wished.

"Good morning, ma'am," Beth said warmly. "How may I help you?"

The woman peered closely at her, the corners of her lips turning into a faint smile. She was younger than Beth had first thought; barely more than thirty, perhaps.

Beth shifted under her gaze. She felt as though she was being scrutinised, though the woman's eyes were undeniably warm.

"Good morning," the woman said after what felt like an eternal pause. She shook herself out of a daze. "A gown," she said, as though she had suddenly remembered what had brought her to this place. "I'd like a gown made. A day dress, if you please."

Beth hesitated. This beautifully dressed woman wanted her to make her an entire gown? She could hardly believe it. Surely someone with her wealth had a whole bevvy of dressmakers at her disposal. Why would she choose Beth as her seamstress? Still, chosen Beth she had, and she was not going to waste this opportunity.

"A day dress," she said, finding her voice. "Yes, of course. Do you have a pattern you would like me to follow?"

The woman tilted her head, her dark curls tickling her cheek. "I've no pattern," she said vaguely.

Beth hesitated. She eyed the voluminous gown the woman was wearing. She wore a wide crinoline, her skirts decorated with layers of flouncing. Her neckline was low, and she wore a delicate lace chemisette.

"In a similar style, perhaps?" Beth asked. She had never before had a customer with so few demands and was slightly taken aback by her approach.

"Yes, I think so," said the woman. "That would be just fine."

Beth nodded, scrawling details in the notebook she kept behind the counter. "And the colour?"

The woman paused again, her eyes on Beth. "Whatever you think best. Blue, perhaps. Or green?"

Beth couldn't hold back a smile. "Whatever I think best?"

"Yes," said the woman, evidently a little flustered. "I'm sure you've much more of a head for these things than I do. Being a seamstress and all."

Beth paused, a smile on her lips. Perhaps the woman was right. After all, she had been stitching clothing almost her entire life. Surely she had picked up a few pieces of knowledge along the way. She had become so used to hearing Mr Whitaker bark insults that the thought of acknowledging her skills felt utterly foreign.

Beth thought back to the empty storeroom and her heart sank. "I'm afraid our fabric supplies are rather low at present. We may not have the stock to create the kind of gown you are… accustomed to."

The woman nodded, clearly unperturbed. "And if I were to pay in advance? You could acquire the necessary fabrics?"

Beth swallowed. "Yes, ma'am. I certainly could."

"Very good." The woman reached into a finely embroidered purse and handed Beth a pouch heavy with coin. "This will be suitable, I assume?"

Beth glanced inside the pouch. It was more money than she had seen in a long time. She had best keep it with her at all times, she decided. There was no way she was going to let Mr Whitaker get his hands on this.

She managed a nod. "Thank you, ma'am. I will be able to purchase you the finest silk with this. I will make you a gown with which you will be most happy."

The woman smiled broadly. "Wonderful." She reached into her purse again and produced a crumpled piece of paper. "My measurements," she said.

Beth looked down at the page. The numbers were written in a small, neat hand that she felt instinctively belonged to the woman herself rather than to any lady's maid.

She looked up, meeting her eyes. Again she felt the intense gaze of the woman. She felt an odd urge to stare back. Swallowing heavily, she pulled her eyes away.

"Thank you," Beth said finally, nodding to the page. "I shall begin work immediately."

A faint frown darkened the woman's face. "You run this place all on your own?"

Beth glanced down. "Well... I... this is Mr Whitaker's shop," she managed. "But he doesn't work much anymore." Her voice came out softer than she had intended, and she felt a sudden flush of guilt. She knew Mr Whitaker would punish her severely if he discovered she had been speaking of him.

"I see," said the woman. "And this Mr Whitaker,

does he treat you well otherwise?" She shook her head a little. "Forgive me," she said hurriedly. "It is not my place to ask." A wide smile broke out across her face and Beth could tell it was forced. "When might I return for my new gown?"

"Perhaps next Friday?" she offered. "You may come for a fitting?"

The woman's face relaxed a little and her smile became warm and genuine. "Next Friday would be perfect. Thank you."

Beth took the accounts book out from under the desk, along with the nib pen and ink. She held it towards the woman. "Will you write your name and details, ma'am?"

"Of course." She dipped the pen in the inkpot and wrote in a flowery hand.

Lady Caroline Speers.

Beth's heart skipped. *Nobility?!* She had known this client had money, but she had not expected this. She pushed the book aside, trying not to show her excitement. Beth frowned to herself. She knew little about the nobility but was well aware that ladies of the upper class did not roam about the city on their own. Where was Lady Caroline's lady's maid? Beth pushed the thought away. Such things were none of her business. All that mattered was that she fashion

Lady Caroline a fine gown and secure her repeat custom.

She smiled broadly. "Thank you, my lady," she said, unable to keep the tremor from her voice. "I shall have your new gown ready for a fitting next Friday."

Lady Caroline smiled. "I very much look forward to it."

And as she swept out of the shop in a flurry of voluminous skirts, Beth realised she was looking forward to it as well.

* * *

That evening, Beth had a smile on her face as she locked the shop and tidied the counter. Lady Caroline had been in her head all day, and the coins she had provided for the purchase of the silk heavy in Beth's pocket.

But it wasn't just about the money, Beth realised. There was something else about the mysterious Lady Caroline that she was unable to place. Perhaps it was her vague approach to dressmaking – as though she had come to the tailor for another reason altogether. Or perhaps it was the way she had looked so carefully at Beth, as though she were trying to memorise every inch of her. Whatever it was, Beth was determined to find out.

She made her way upstairs, her stomach groaning with hunger. Their pantry was woefully empty, Beth remembered, her shoulders sinking. Still, once she had finished the new gown for Lady Caroline, they would be able to afford a little more than watery broth.

"Elizabeth!" Mr Whitaker barked.

Beth stiffened. She opened the door to his bedroom and poked her head inside. These days she could rely on Mr Whitaker to be in one of three places: the tavern, the gambling halls or sprawled upon his bed. Beth could hardly remember the last time she'd seen him set foot in the shop.

She found him stretched out on top of his bed clothes, still wearing his coat and muddy boots. His unruly grey hair was tangled over the pillow. The room reeked of whisky and tobacco.

He peered at her through narrowed eyes. "Where are today's takings?"

Beth dug into her pocket and handed over the few coins she had earned that day, keeping Lady Caroline's money safely hidden. Mr Whitaker looked down at them. "Is this all?"

"Yes, sir. I'm afraid there were few sales today.

But—" she stopped abruptly. She would not tell Mr Whitaker about the wealthy woman's visit. The new gown Beth was making would earn her a handsome sum and they could not afford to have Mr Whitaker drink it away.

"But I'll try harder tomorrow," she finished.

Mr Whitaker snorted in response. "I want my supper," he said. "And if you know what's good for you, you'll put some damn meat in my stew tonight."

Beth left Mr Whitaker's room, closing the door behind her. She hurried to her bedroom and dropped to her knees beside the bed. She pulled a coin from the pouch Lady Caroline had given her and used it to prise up the loose floorboard beside her bed. She tucked the pouch into the cavity. She smiled to herself as she replaced the floorboard. Safe from the gambling hall and the tavern. Safe from Mr Whitaker's eyes.

CHAPTER 10

Beth set to work at once designing the gown for the mysterious Lady Caroline. She hunched over her table in the storeroom, designing a deep V-necked bodice and bell sleeves, culminating in a voluminous layered skirt. She stared down at the design, trying to picture Lady Caroline wearing it. Was such a dress fitting for a member of the nobility? Beth had never made clothing for someone so high up in society before. She felt a sudden flush of doubt. What if she made a fool of herself? What if the gown was unwearable? What if Lady Caroline refused to pay?

Beth shook her fears away and tried to concentrate on the design. She was determined that it would be her best work yet. If she could secure the ongoing patronage of such a wealthy woman, it would make life far easier for her and Mr Whitaker. But she could not deny there was more to it than that.

She had looked at Beth so intently. When last had anyone paid her so much attention? When last had someone given her more than just a passing glance?

In the afternoon, Beth went to the market to purchase a roll of dark green silk for Lady Caroline's dress. She felt a smile on her lips as she hurried back to the shop. She was sure Lady Caroline had plenty of friends in the nobility. Perhaps after she saw this fine gown, she might make referral beneficial to Beth and Mr Whitaker's business.

Beth laughed at herself. Earlier that day she had been full of doubts, and now here she was imagining herself as a seamstress to all the wealthy ladies of London.

She hurried back to the shop, hoping Mr Whitaker had not noticed her absence. Inside was silent, and she heaved a sigh of relief. No doubt Mr Whitaker was either off at the gambling halls or sleeping off the previous night's excesses. She did not want him to know about the commission from Lady Caroline at all, she realised. She didn't know why. Perhaps it was so she might have the option of keeping the money hidden beneath the floorboard, saving it from being gambled away. Or perhaps there was more to it. Beth didn't quite understand her reason. She just knew she wanted to keep Lady Caroline's visit a secret.

BETH WORKED TIRELESSLY throughout the week, cutting and stitching until her fingers were raw and her back ached. She had designed the dress herself, using the gown Lady Caroline had been wearing as a starting point, then adding subtle detail to the bodice and neckline. She had even added delicate embroidery work to the skirts that would only be noticeable on close inspection.

Working on the gown filled Beth with joy. Not only was she getting paid handsomely for the job, but this was also undoubtedly the most beautiful creation by her hand alone.

The following Friday, Lady Caroline returned. Beth had stayed up late finishing the gown and it hung in waiting on a hook behind the counter.

She watched through the window as Lady Caroline climbed from a coach outside the shop and made her way to the door. Once again, she was unaccompanied. Beth's heart began to pound. The bell tinkled as Lady Caroline stepped inside.

Her dark gaze fell upon the dress. "Oh," she gushed. "Is that for me?"

Beth hesitated. She couldn't tell if the exclamation was one of pleasure or disappointment. The pounding in her chest intensified. "Yes," she said, suddenly shy. "Do you like it?" Her voice felt trapped in her throat.

"It's perfect." Lady Caroline smiled warmly. "Utterly perfect." She hovered beside the counter. "May I feel the fabric?"

"Of course?"

Beth laid the gown over the bench and let Lady Caroline run her finger along the neat stitching. "This is exquisite work," she said, bending over to examine the embroidery in the folds of the skirt. "You did this all yourself?"

Beth felt the colour rising in her cheeks. "Yes, ma'am. I'm so pleased you like it." She peered up at the woman, suddenly overcome with shyness. "Perhaps you might try it on? And I can make the final alterations?"

Lady Caroline clutched the dress to herself. "I've not brought my maid," she said unnecessarily. She gestured to the row of tiny buttons down her back. "Perhaps you might…?"

Beth fought the urge to ask her why she saw fit to travel alone. Such a thing was frowned upon by the nobility, surely. *It's none of my business,* she reminded herself. Instead, she said, "Of course. I'd be happy to help."

Beth gestured to the dressing screen behind which her clients changed. She hung the dress on the hook on the wall. Lady Caroline stood motionless in front of her as Beth worked at the intricate row of buttons at her back. She helped Lady Caroline lift her day dress over her head and slide on the silk gown. Lady Caroline smoothed the fabric over her broad crinoline, while Beth stood behind her, her fingers darting over the row of tiny hooks at the back.

"Oh," Lady Caroline exclaimed when Beth stepped back, having fastened the final hook, "it's a perfect fit. What a wonderful job you've done." She turned to face the mirror, running her hand over the silky green planes of the dress. "Yes," she said. "Perfect."

Beth stood at her side, peering into the mirror to examine the way the dress tickled the floor. She smiled to herself, pleased with the effectiveness of the subtle embroidery.

"I need to finish the hem," she said, taking her box of pins from her apron pocket and kneeling at Lady Caroline's feet. Expertly she pinned the hem a half-inch off the floor.

She climbed to her feet, smoothing her apron. "I can have it finished for you tomorrow if you wish."

Lady Caroline's smile broadened. "Thank you," she said, "Miss…?"

"Thursday," said Beth. "Beth Thursday."

Something flickered in Lady Caroline's eyes. "Beth," she repeated. "For Elizabeth?"

Beth nodded. "Yes, my lady."

Lady Caroline flashed her a quick smile, then turned, hiding her eyes from Beth. "Please," she said. "Help me with the hooks."

Beth helped Lady Caroline out of the gown, hanging it back behind the counter for hemming.

"Thank you, Miss Thursday," said Lady Caroline as she emerged from behind the dressing screen. "Your work is just beautiful. I look forward to receiving the finished gown tomorrow."

CHAPTER 11

*L*ady Caroline returned to the shop several more times, each time commissioning a new item of clothing. Each time she arrived alone, with little more than a vague idea of what she wanted for her piece. Hunched over the lamp in the storeroom, Beth designed and stitched day dresses and evening gowns, petticoats, and even a pair of evening gloves.

And with each new garment, the pouch beneath the floorboards grew heavier. This week she had even managed to add beef to her and Mr Whitaker's stew. Just enough for a little sustenance. Not enough for the master of the house to begin asking questions.

In the back of her mind, Beth knew she and Mr

Whitaker could not go on like this forever. One day soon, Mr Whitaker would gamble away the last of their money, or else his drinking would claim his life. And when that happened, she would need to be ready. Lady Caroline's money was something of a life raft. It would ensure she could keep a roof over her head if – or when – the Whitakers' tailoring shop ceased to exist.

Each time Beth slipped another coin into the pouch beneath the floorboards, she felt a faint pang of guilt. Was this theft? She did not own the shop, after all. She was just Mr Whitaker's apprentice. Surely keeping the proceeds to herself was highly illegal.

But then she would rub her aching fingers and remember that Mr Whitaker had not helped her in the shop for years. She had ceased being his apprentice years ago. The shop would have ceased to exist long ago, had she not held it together. As for these gowns she so carefully stitched for Lady Caroline, Beth was determined to receive a little compensation.

One day, as she laced Lady Caroline's new gown for a fitting, she found herself blurting out: "The coins you give me. I hide a few of them under the floorboards in my room." The issue had been roiling inside her head for weeks. "Do you think me a thief?"

Lady Caroline didn't speak at once and Beth felt the colour rise in her cheeks. She could hardly believe she had dared ask such a thing.

It was true, over the past few visits she and Lady Caroline had started speaking more and more. Beth, who felt inexplicably comfortable around her wealthy customer, had taken to asking her question after question, desperate to know more about the mysterious world of the nobility.

Lady Caroline had told her about her family's vast manor house in Chelsea, and about all her brothers and sisters. She had spoken of the endless parade of governesses and tutors in her childhood growing up, and of the balls she had attended in the pursuit of finding a husband.

"And?" Beth had asked impatiently, desperate to know who Lady Caroline had married.

Lady Caroline gave a small smile. "And… I found no husband. Perhaps the men deemed me unsuitable…"

Beth frowned. How could Lady Caroline be deemed unsuitable? She was so warm and open, and beautiful…

"Or," she continued, "perhaps there was a part of

me that did not wish to be chosen. Perhaps this part of me did all it could to keep the suitors at bay."

Beth smiled. She felt as though she were being let into some deep secret, one which few people were privy to.

And so today she had felt comfortable enough to blurt out the truth about hiding the coins. Yet now her cheeks were burning with shame. Lady Caroline sharing her secrets was one thing. After all, she was the client, and a wealthy, upper class one at that. She could behave however she wished, Beth decided. But it was hardly fitting behaviour for a seamstress to blurt out her most shameful secret. And to a member of the nobility! She could hardly have behaved more unprofessionally.

"Forgive me," she murmured, her cheeks blazing. "I should never…"

But Lady Caroline turned to face her. "Why do you hide them?" she asked Beth gently.

Beth looked at her feet in shame. "I don't want Mr Whitaker to have them," she said. "He is careless with our money. I need to keep a little aside. I…"

Lady Caroline pressed soft hands to Beth's shoulders. "If it was up to me, my darling, you would have every penny from these gowns. After all, you are the one who has done all the work, are you not?"

Beth gave a small smile, lowering her eyes. "Yes, but—"

"Then you have every right to be paid accordingly." She strutted out from behind the dressing screen, making Beth skip to catch up with her. "This Mr Whitaker," she said. "What does he spend the money on? Drink? Is that it?"

Beth hesitated. Speaking about Mr Whitaker like this felt something of a betrayal. But how desperately she needed to share the weight upon her shoulders. How desperately she needed to tell someone about all that had gone on in the years since Mrs Whitaker's death.

"Drink, yes," she admitted, eyes down. "And he likes to frequent the gambling houses." She swallowed heavily. "I fear one day soon we will lose the shop. And unless I put the coins aside, I will be out on the streets with nothing."

Lady Caroline's dark eyes narrowed in anger. "I will not have the money I give you for these gowns frittered away at the gambling houses." Though she had already paid in full for her latest orders, Lady Caroline dug into her purse and held out a few coins. "Give this to Mr Whitaker. Tell him it was all you earned today. Keep the rest for yourself."

Beth shook her head vehemently. "No," she

gushed, looking down at the coins. "I couldn't. I…" Her cheeks blazed and she cursed herself for having raised the issue. But at the same time, something flared inside her. No one had fought for her like this since Mrs Whitaker had died.

"Thank you," she said, calmly. "But I truly can't."

Lady Caroline nodded, slipping the coins back into her purse. "I understand," she said. "I apologise if I caused you discomfort."

Beth shook her head dismissively.

Lady Caroline opened her mouth to speak, then stopped.

Beth paused. "Is something wrong?"

Lady Caroline shook her head. "No, no… I just…" She swallowed heavily, knotting her gloved fingers together. Beth had never seen her look so thoroughly uncertain of herself. "Perhaps instead of accepting the money, you might permit me to take you to lunch tomorrow. As a way of thanking you for all the work you have done for me of late."

Beth's heart quickened. Had she truly been invited to lunch with a member of the nobility? Such a thing hardly seemed possible.

"If you'd rather not, I—"

"No," Beth said hurriedly. "I would love that. Very

much." She grinned, despite the nerves that had begun to roil inside her. "Thank you."

Lady Caroline's face broke into a broad smile. "Wonderful. I shall have the coach come for you at twelve. Is that suitable?"

Beth nodded.

"Oh, and Miss Thursday…" Lady Caroline reached into her purse again and pulled out a calling card. She slipped it into Beth's hand. Beth looked down at the dark swirl of writing.

"If Mr Whitaker causes you trouble, or if there is anything else you need, you may find me at this address."

Beth swallowed hard, a sudden, inexplicable rush of emotion tightening her throat.

"Thank you."

CHAPTER 12

*C*aroline Speers ran her finger along the tiny stitching on the hem of her new gown. Her head was full of Beth Thursday, as it had been since the first day she had set foot in that tailor's shop.

In truth, her head had been full of the girl for the last seventeen years. That precious baby girl who had been torn from her arms before she was an hour old.

"Elizabeth," Caroline had sobbed. "Her name is Elizabeth."

It had brought her more than a little happiness to find the men who had taken her had at least given the child the name her mother had chosen.

"I was brought to the workhouse on a Thursday,"

Beth had told her that day, while she had pinned the hem on her latest creation. "That's where I earned my name."

Yes, Caroline remembered distantly. It had been a Thursday. Simultaneously the happiest and most devastating day of her life. The day she had held her baby daughter to her chest, only to have her torn away.

Caroline had been just sixteen when she had discovered herself with child. She had been young and foolish; infatuated by the broad-shouldered, dark-eyed marquess she had danced with at the spring ball. Back then, she had assumed she, like every other woman of her station, would marry. And she wanted no one but the marquess as her husband. She could hardly believe it when he asked her father's permission to call on her after the ball.

With each afternoon tea, each walk in the park, Caroline became more and more besotted. The marquess, at twenty, seemed endlessly wise, impossibly sophisticated. Caroline felt herself completely unworthy of his attentions. Each time she saw him, her joy was tempered by a fear that he would realise her plainness and lack of place in this world. And so, when he told her to creep from her father's townhouse and pay a clandestine visit to him, Caroline had found herself agreeing.

With nervous excitement, she had slipped through the dark manor and run the lamplit streets of London to the marquess's townhouse. And it was with nervous excitement that she allowed him to do the unthinkable in the opulence of his bed-chamber.

Caroline had crept back to the manor, her heart thumping and her skin hot. Surely now the marquess's proposal would be forthcoming. Surely it would be just a matter of weeks before he made her his wife.

But Caroline did not hear another word from the marquess. His silence was brutal, and she took to her bed-chamber, feigning illness, unable to face reality.

But when the illness became real and her courses failed to appear, Caroline knew she could no longer ignore reality. She could curl up in her bed-chamber all she wanted, but she knew in a matter of months there would be a child. And unless the marquess accepted her as his wife – and did so with urgency – the shame upon Caroline's family would be endless.

She asked her maid for a pen and paper and wrote a blunt and honest letter to the marquess, telling him everything. She pleaded with him for the marriage proposal that would save her from crippling shame.

She received no reply.

In desperation, Caroline wrote to the marquess two more times, unable to think of anything else to do. She was not surprised by his silence.

Finally, she decided she had little choice but to admit to her family what she had done. Already, her corset was unbearably tight, and she knew it was only a matter of days before her lady's maid discovered her secret.

Caroline was shaking with fear as she made her way into the parlour to confess all to her parents. She had heard countless stories of what happened to unwed mothers – shipped off to convents, thrown out on the streets, their children taken away...

No, she told herself. None of these would happen to her. Despite his hard shell, her father was a good man. He had always treated her and her siblings well. Had always been fair, had always listened to their problems and done his best to solve them. Surely, he would forgive her this mistake. And somehow, he would find a way to make it right.

Caroline tapped nervously on the door of the parlour.

"Yes?" the Earl called.

She stepped into the room, swallowing a violent wave of nausea. Her parents were sitting in armchairs in front of the fire, wine glasses in their hands.

"Father," she began. "Mother… There's something I need to tell you…"

EARLY THE NEXT MORNING, Caroline climbed into a coach with her father seated on the bench opposite her. His eyes were dark and unforgiving.

Somewhere in the back of her mind, Caroline knew she had expected this. Despite her attempts at convincing herself otherwise, she had expected to be carted away once she confessed her shameful secret. After all, her family was respected and revered among the London nobility. How could they abide an unwed mother beneath their roof? They could not know the shame of keeping the likes of Caroline among them.

She knew she had been foolish to think there could have been any other outcome than this.

Caroline pulled her shawl tightly around her shoulders as she huddled into the corner of the carriage. A part of her thought to apologise to her father again. But what good would it do? There was an anger in the

Earl's eyes she had never seen before. Anger that bordered on hatred. Caroline knew nothing she said would improve the situation. She turned her eyes away from him, stilted silence hanging in the air.

She was to be taken to a convent, Caroline supposed. Give birth to her child away from the prying eyes of London's high society. Her mother and father would tell everyone she was unwell. They would feign a look of deep concern as they told the world their daughter had been taken to a sanatorium by the seaside in the hope she would recover.

Yes, they would say sadly, *we expect her to be away for some months.*

And then what? What would happen when the baby arrived? Caroline couldn't bear to think of it. All she wanted was to live a life with her child by her side.

She knew her parents would never allow such a thing. If they had their way, the child would be scooped from her arms the moment it arrived, never to know its mother.

No. Caroline would not have it. She ran a protective hand over her belly. This child was hers and she would not let anyone separate them. Ever. It didn't matter if she had to live on the streets. Somehow, she would find a way. And she had months in a convent to come up with a plan.

Caroline didn't look back as the carriage pulled away from her father's townhouse. Perhaps this was a life she would never return to. Perhaps she would never see this house again. Perhaps she would not see her mother or father, or her siblings. The thought made tears prick her eyes. Despite the way her parents had handled her news, she loved them both dearly. And she had always been close to her brothers and sisters. Losing them would break her heart. But if that was what she had to do to be with her son or daughter, that was what she would do. Nothing was more important than her child.

She closed her eyes, listening to the rhythmic clatter of hooves against the cobbled street, not looking up until the coach began to slow. It rattled through high iron gates and along the wide path that stretched through an endless manicured garden. Trees grew in neat rows and men and women were dotted across the lawns, many dressed in drab grey clothing.

Caroline straightened. The building ahead looked nothing like a convent. It was almost as vast as the garden, three storeys high and dotted with narrow windows. The coach slowed to a halt, the wheels crunching on the stone path.

"Father?" she coughed. "What is this place?"

Her father pressed his lips into a thin white line. "Just get out of the coach, Caroline."

She clenched her hands into fists, fear shooting through her. She stayed motionless on the bench. The coachman opened the door, offering her his hand. Caroline's eyes pleaded with her father. "Father, please. Just tell me what's happening."

The Earl climbed out of the coach. "I'm sorry, Caroline," he said stiffly. "It has to be this way. You brought this on yourself when you saw fit to shame our family."

He took her arm firmly, forcing her out of the carriage. As her feet hit the ground, Caroline caught sight of the brass nameplate sign above the main door of the building.

Bethlem Royal Hospital.

Her blood ran cold. She knew well of Bethlem. Knew exactly what manner of patients they admitted.

"Father?" she coughed. "The Bedlam? Really? An asylum? A *madhouse?*" A sudden fear seized her, and she turned to run.

The Earl snatched her wrist, preventing her from

disappearing. He kept a hand firmly around the top of her arm, marching her towards the gates.

Caroline tried to pull away. Her heart was racing, her skin prickling with sweat. "No, Father, please. There must be some other way."

The Earl stopped walking and turned to glare at her. "There is no other way, Caroline. Do you not understand how greatly you have shamed this family? I think of no other reason than you must be ill. Madness must have struck you to cause such dishonourable behaviour."

"No," Caroline said stiffly. "No. I'm not mad. They'll see that. They'll see that and they'll release me."

The Earl chuckled humourlessly. "I'm paying them far too much for them to allow that to happen. As far as these people are concerned, you're a jilted young woman who was driven mad when she found herself with child."

FOR SIX MONTHS, Caroline stayed locked within the walls of Bethlem Asylum, listening to the moans and cries of the patients around her.

At night, she lay alone in her whitewashed cell of

a room, a hand on her belly, feeling her child move inside her.

Everything would be all right, she told herself. Somehow, everything would be all right. She had no idea how. But convincing herself she and her child would somehow get through this together was the only thing that kept her afloat.

When Elizabeth had arrived on a rainy Thursday evening, the midwife had placed her in Caroline's arms. And for the briefest of moments, things had truly felt all right. She and her daughter were together. Together in the asylum, yes, but somehow she would find a way to change that.

But then Doctor Miller, the head physician, had strode forth and ordered an attendant to take the child from her arms.

"It's the way things must be," he had said calmly, barely audible over Caroline's shrieking. And: "Your father has wished it."

A YEAR after Elizabeth's birth, the Earl brought his daughter home from the asylum. Caroline was surprised. She had expected to spend the rest of her life between the whitewashed walls of Bethlem as punishment for her terrible decisions.

As she rode home in the carriage beside her father, a part of her ached to ask him why he had seen fit to release her. Had he grown tired of paying for Caroline's unnecessary treatment? Had he decided she had been punished enough? Perhaps her mother had intervened. But as much as she longed to know his reasons, Caroline found herself utterly unable to speak to the Earl.

The very sight of him made her jaw clench in anger. If she were to utter a word to him, she would either break down into tears or explode with rage. Whatever his reasons, she realised, she didn't care. She had no desire to speak to her father ever again.

The Earl set to work finding his wayward daughter a husband.

"It's time you put the past behind you, Caroline," he said firmly. "Try and make something of the rest of your life."

Caroline was gripped with anger. How could she marry? How could she start a new life, have a new family, when her daughter was out in the world somewhere? A bitter hatred for her father burned inside her.

Her father forced her to attend balls and soirees, garden parties and afternoon teas. The parade of suitors blended into one, with not a single man doing anything to lift Caroline from the grief she still felt over her loss of Elizabeth. She spoke only when spoken to, refused to dance, and found no joy in her once-beloved piano.

Despite the endless array of suitors, no marriage proposal was forthcoming. Perhaps word of her incarceration at the asylum had somehow gotten out. Perhaps even word of her illegitimate child. After all, she had told the marquess. Perhaps someone had found one of her pleading letters.

But Caroline knew it was far more likely that it was her new dour personality that had turned potential husbands away. Losing Elizabeth had caused her to sink into a deep melancholy and that, she knew, was not something a man wanted in a wife.

Finally, her father gave up. After all, the Earl of Derbyshire had two other daughters and three sons. As far as he was concerned, finding a husband for Caroline was not worth the trouble. Let her become a sad and lonely spinster. Wasn't that what she deserved?

With her father's attentions firmly off her, Caroline threw herself into searching for her daughter. But where was she to even begin? She had no idea where Elizabeth had been taken. Had she been adopted by a childless couple? Sent to an orphanage? The workhouse? Was she still in London, or had she been carted off to another part of the country? Or even another part of the world? The not knowing, Caroline realised, was by far the worst. Perhaps being separated from her child would be bearable if she knew Elizabeth was safe and loved. But all she had was uncertainty.

Her search, Caroline knew, had to start at Bethlem Asylum. The attendants there had been the ones to take Elizabeth; the ones who knew where she was. How she would contact them, Caroline had no thought. If she wrote directly to the asylum, she knew there was every chance Miller would be notified, and he, in turn, would tell his patron, the Earl. That was a risk Caroline could not afford to take.

Instead, she made her way to the asylum, having firmly told her lady's maid she did not require her company. Caroline stood across the road from the main gates, waiting for a familiar face to emerge. There was an endless number of attendants at the asylum, she knew and waiting to catch a glimpse of the nurse who had taken Elizabeth away felt like an impossible task.

But she waited. For days, weeks, months, she returned to the asylum every day before finally catching a glimpse of the attendant she had so desperately sought out.

Caroline hurried after the middle-aged woman. "Please. Wait."

The woman turned in surprise. There was a glimmer of recognition in her eye as she looked at Caroline.

Caroline straightened her shoulders and lifted her chin. Each day she came to the asylum, she wore her finest clothing and bonnet with her hair neatly pinned, and her shoes polished. Looking as elegant and composed as possible, she knew, would be crucial in determining the information she needed.

"You remember me," she said to the attendant.

The woman nodded. "Yes. Lady Caroline." She pressed her lips into a thin white line, clearly uncomfortable at being accosted in this way.

"My daughter, Elizabeth, was born in the asylum three years ago," said Caroline. "You took her from my arms." She tried to keep her voice even. Despite the anger she felt at the attendant, she knew the woman had just been doing her job. She was not to blame for the separation of mother and daughter. "I need to know where my child was taken."

The attendant began to walk hurriedly. "You know I can't tell you that."

"Of course you can," Caroline said sharply. "I'm her *mother*!"

"I'm sorry for your loss," the woman said, not looking at her. "But you need to move past it."

"How can I do that?" Caroline cried. "My daughter was stolen from me!" She grabbed the woman's arm, her anger tearing free. "Now tell me where you took her!"

The woman pulled away sharply, her eyes flashing indignantly. "Get away from me," she hissed. "Or I'll go for the police."

Caroline swallowed heavily, tears welling in her eyes. "I'm sorry. Please. Just tell me what you know. No one will ever need know it was you who told me."

The woman shook her head. "I've no idea where your child was taken. After I took her from your room, I gave her to one of the groundskeepers and instructed him to find a home for her."

Caroline's heart quickened. "Who is this groundskeeper? Where can I find him?"

The attendant shook her head and began to walk again. "I'm sorry," she said, not sounding sorry at all. "The man died six months ago."

. . .

CAROLINE WROTE letter after letter to every orphanage and foundling hospital in the country. She received few replies, none of which had any information on Elizabeth. As her search stretched out over the years, Caroline tried to imagine what her daughter would look like, tried to imagine how she would behave. What did she do with her life? Was she being cared for? Did she have work? A family? Had she found herself another mother? Caroline didn't know if the thought comforted her or filled her with grief.

Finally, after years and years of unsuccessful searching, she sought the help of an old-fashioned thief-taker who was skilled in investigating crimes. He promised her his silence in exchange for a large fee. And he discovered that Elizabeth had not been taken to another country. Nor had she been sent to an orphanage or a foundling hospital. Instead, swathed in a thin grey blanket, she had simply been taken across the river from Bethlem Asylum to the Southwark Workhouse. Hidden in plain sight, in the most obvious place.

Caroline strode into the workhouse master's office and planted a pouch of coins on his desk.

"I need information about my daughter," she said,

looking the man in the eye. "She was brought here seventeen years ago as an infant."

The master picked up the pouch and glanced inside. Then he looked back at Caroline. After a moment of consideration, he reached into his drawer and pulled out an enormous leather-bound register.

"Your daughter's name?"

Caroline swallowed. She had no idea what name her child had been given. *Elizabeth*, she had shrieked as they had taken her child from her arms. But she knew there was every chance her daughter had been given another name.

She looked squarely at the master. "I don't know what name she was given. But she would have been brought here on or just after the 18th of June 1837."

The master nodded.

As she watched him turn through the pages of the ledger, Caroline thought of her father. What would he do if he discovered she was hunting down her illegitimate daughter? Such a thing would bring unfathomable shame to the family. Caroline knew the Earl would punish her severely if he caught her, her allowance would be gone. Perhaps he'd even send her back to the Bedlam.

She pushed the thought away. She was worried

about nothing, she told herself. After all, her father had barely paid her a scrap of notice since she had refused to take a husband. They had barely exchanged a word in years. Despite living in the same Chelsea townhouse, Caroline would go days, sometimes even weeks, without seeing him. She knew her father did all he could to forget he had a shameful spinster living under his roof.

She pressed her shoulders back defiantly as she watched the workhouse master turn the pages of his ledger. She was closer to finding her daughter now than she had ever been. She was not going to let the fear of her father stop her now.

"Ah," the master said finally, his voice snapping Caroline from her thoughts. "Here we are. Elizabeth Thursday. Arrived at the workhouse as an infant on the evening of the 18th of June 1837. The only entry for three days for an infant. She must be the child you seek."

Caroline's heart began to race, and she gripped the edge of the table to steady herself.

Elizabeth...

She felt a sudden knot in her stomach. "What happened to her?" she managed. "Is she…"

Though she had not let herself follow the thought through, she knew there was every chance her child might not have survived. What would she do if she was to learn that her precious Elizabeth was dead? How would she go on? Without the prospect of seeing her child again, what did Caroline have to live for?

The master squinted as though trying to decipher his own handwriting. Caroline fought the urge to shake an answer from him and instead produced another small purse of coins.

"The girl was apprenticed to a Mr James Whitaker," he said finally after eying the purse for a few seconds.

Caroline let out her breath, a violent rush of relief flooding her.

"This was nine years ago."

"And where can I find this Mr Whitaker?" she asked, trying to keep her voice steady.

The master hesitated, nodding to the coins she had placed on the desk. "This is most irregular, you understand?"

Caroline pressed her lips together and dug into her purse. She sat another handful of shillings on the table, the last of the money she had on her person.

"He owns a tailor's shop in Kensington," said the master, scrawling the address on a piece of paper.

"At least he did eight years ago. I can't guarantee you'll still find him here."

Caroline looked down at his scrawled handwriting. Her heart was pounding in her chest. At last, after all these years she had an address. She was going to find her daughter.

* * *

CAROLINE STARED into the mirror as her lady's maid fastened the buttons at the back of her gown. Her stomach was in knots. In less than an hour, she was to take Elizabeth to lunch. And Caroline planned to tell her everything. The thought brought her a frisson of excitement, but also a considerable amount of fear.

She and Beth had gotten along well, but how would the girl react when she learned the truth? Would she forgive her mother for abandoning her? Would she understand that Caroline was afforded no choice? There was no guarantee of it, of course.

Caroline had heard stories of the workhouse. Knew children were put to work the moment they could walk. Knew they were badly fed; knew they were crammed into beds like animals in cages. She knew of the miserable start Beth would have had to her life and it made something ache inside her.

And this Mr Whitaker? From what little Beth had told her, her life with him was not likely to have been much better.

Yes, Caroline thought sadly, Beth would be well within her rights not to forgive her.

But after seventeen years of searching and longing, she at least had to try.

CHAPTER 13

*B*eth opened Mr Whitaker's bedroom door a crack and peeked inside. He was slumped across his bed, snoring loudly, his big toe poking out a hole in his stockings. An empty liquor bottle lay on its side next to the bed. Gin? Scotch? She couldn't be sure and didn't care.

Beth had debated telling Mr Whitaker about her lunch with Lady Caroline, reasoning that he ought to know she would not be in the shop. She had even considered asking him to man the counter for a few hours. But there was little point, she realised. He would sleep through most of the day and would likely not even notice she was gone. Besides, she was not about to run the risk of him forbidding her to go. When in her life would she have the chance to join a noblewoman for a meal?

She pulled the door closed on Mr Whitaker and returned to her room. She stood in front of her cupboard, peering at the row of dresses. Despite having little money, the wardrobe was full of finely stitched gowns made by Beth from the tailor shop's offcuts. Her collection of dresses was her most prized possession.

She stood for several long moments, deciding what best to wear. She had no idea where Lady Caroline was planning to take her, but Beth knew she most definitely ought to look her best.

She decided on a dark blue woollen gown that buttoned to her neck. She ran a brush through her tangle of curls, then carefully plaited and pinned her hair. She peered at her reflection and smiled. She looked nowhere near as glamorous as Lady Caroline, who swept through the streets in voluminous crinoline, but at least she might not be mistaken for her lady's maid.

Beth peeked in at Mr Whitaker one last time then, satisfied he would sleep the day away, she made her way downstairs to wait for Lady Caroline.

. . .

Precisely at midday, the bell above the door rang and Lady Caroline stepped into the shop. She was wearing the dark green afternoon dress Beth had first designed for her, a feathered bonnet perched on top of her dark curls.

Beth felt a sudden swell of nerves. Where did Lady Caroline plan to take her? Would she fit in? The workhouse matron and Mrs Whitaker had all done their best to instil in Beth good manners, but she felt nonetheless that her etiquette would be lacking in the eyes of the upper class.

At the sight of her, Lady Caroline's face broke into a warm smile and Beth's nerves vanished.

Lady Caroline reached for Beth's hands and gave them a gentle squeeze. "I'm so pleased to see you, my dear. I've been so looking forward to today. I truly want to do something special to thank you for all your hard work." Her words came out in a flurry.

Was Lady Caroline herself nervous, Beth wondered? For what reason?

"Will Mr Whitaker mind your absence from the shop this afternoon?" she asked. "Your customers will miss you?"

Beth shook her head. "There's no need to bother ourselves with Mr Whitaker."

And my only customer these days is you, she thought with a wry smile.

"He won't punish you?" Lady Caroline asked, concern in her dark eyes.

Beth shook her head. "He'll not even notice me gone. I'm sure of it."

Lady Caroline smiled. "Good. My coachman is waiting," she said. "Shall we?"

Beth nodded, smiling. She locked up the shop and followed Lady Caroline out to the waiting carriage.

The coachman opened the door and offered them his hand, helping them into the carriage one at a time. Beth slid onto the soft padded bench seat, sitting opposite Lady Caroline. She looked around the coach in amazement.

The roof was painted cream, with dark floral designs in the corner, the windows hemmed with dark velvet curtains. It was far more luxurious than any cab she had ever been in in the past. Not that she had been in many. With a smile, Beth realised she had never even seen a house as luxurious as this coach. She could stretch out on the bench seats and have the most comfortable sleep of her life.

"The carriage is so beautiful," she gushed as they pulled away from the shop.

Lady Caroline ran a slender finger over the edge of the bench, as though noticing the details of the coach for the first time. "It belongs to my father," she said finally. Her voice was clipped, with a hint of coldness.

Beth knotted her fingers together, regretting her words.

Lady Caroline held her eyes closed for a second, before looking back at Beth with a smile. "I thought we might go to Brown's. It's one of my favourite places to take a meal."

"Brown's?" Beth garbled. "Yes, I..." She knew well of Brown's Hotel, having sewn and mended dresses for ladies who dined there. Once, on her way home from the market, she had even detoured down Albemarle Street so she might catch a glimpse of the place she had so often heard about.

But never had she imagined she might one day be dining there herself.

The carriage slowed to a halt and Beth peered excitedly out the window at the vast white façade of the hotel. Well-dressed men and women were clustered outside the front door, beside a butler in a dark suit and top hat.

"Will this place please you?" asked Lady Caroline.

Beth grinned incredulously. "Of course! I can hardly believe I'm about to eat at such a place."

Lady Caroline's eyes sparkled. "You deserve it, my dear. You've been working so hard for me of late." She looked into her folded hands. "I daresay you've been working hard every day of your life."

Beth swallowed heavily, saying nothing. The coachman clicked the door open and offered his hand first to Lady Caroline, then to Beth.

Beth stared up at the building, her nerves reappearing. She knotted her fingers together awkwardly. Perhaps this was a mistake. She was nothing but an orphan from the workhouse. What right did she have setting foot inside an establishment such this? The patrons would take one look at her and know she didn't belong.

Lady Caroline stood close. "Are you all right?" she asked, frowning.

Beth drew in her breath. "I shouldn't be here," she managed. "I… I don't belong in such an establishment."

To her surprise, Lady Caroline pressed her hands to Beth's shoulders and turned her to face her. "You have every right to be here," she said fervently. "Do you understand me? Never let anyone tell you otherwise."

Beth swallowed heavily, feeling tears prick her eyes. No one had ever spoken to her in a such a way before. No one had ever made her feel so worthwhile. Not even kind Mrs Whitaker.

"All right?"

Beth nodded, her voice trapped in her throat.

Lady Caroline smiled. "Good." She kept Beth's hand pressed into the crook of her arm, their fingers interlaced.

"My table manners," Beth garbled. "I don't know if they are correct… Or if…"

She faded out at the sight of Lady Caroline's smile. "Just copy me, my dear. Everything will be just fine." She caught Beth's eye. "I'm sorry if I have made you feel uncomfortable. It absolutely was not my intention."

But as Beth floated through the elaborately decorated dining room with this glamorous lady at her side, she realised discomfort was not at all what she was feeling.

LUNCH WAS an array of dishes foreign to Beth. Course after course of soups and salmon and pigeon pie appeared on the table, adorned with vegetables and rich creamy sauces. Beth savoured each bite of the decadent luncheon, eating until she could feel her stomach pressing against her corset. She couldn't remember the last time she had not felt hungry. She thought back to the delicious dinners she had cooked with Mrs Whitaker. Even they could not compare to this feast.

She watched wide-eyed as the waiter placed a bowl of meringues and berries in front of her. She felt her mouth water, though she could hardly imagine how she might fit any more food in. Still, she was determined to try.

Lady Caroline picked up her spoon and scooped up a minuscule portion of cream. She had done little but pick at her food all afternoon, Beth had noticed.

"Is everything all right, My Lady?" she asked.

Lady Caroline put the spoon into her mouth and swallowed down the cream. "Yes. Of course. Everything is lovely. I do hope you're enjoying yourself."

Beth gave an airy laugh. "I'm enjoying myself so much! Who would ever have imagined an orphan from the workhouse would end up eating in such a place?"

Lady Caroline didn't share her laughter. Beth saw something pass across her eyes.

"Tell me about the workhouse," Lady Caroline

said, putting down her spoon. Her voice was soft and stilted.

Beth hesitated. It felt odd to be speaking of the workhouse in this lavish place. "What do you wish to know?"

Lady Caroline folded her napkin into a tiny square and squeezed it between her fingers. "Was it dreadful?"

Beth stirred her tea. The workhouse had been challenging, for certain, but would she have described it as dreadful? As a child, she had known nothing else.

"They worked us very hard," she admitted. "And the matron used to scare me. I was afraid she would take me to the master for a beating." She bristled at the memory. "But they kept us fed and warm. I was never lonely." She gave Lady Caroline a small smile. "I know things could have been much worse for me."

Lady Caroline didn't return her smile. She stared into her teacup for a long time, her lips parted as though she wanted to speak, but couldn't find the words.

"It's my fault you had such a childhood," she said after a long silence. Her voice wavered.

Beth frowned. "What do you mean?"

Two tears slid down Lady Caroline's cheeks. She

cleared her throat. "I'm your mother, Beth," she said huskily. She swiped at her tears. "I apologise for the abrupt admission."

Beth's spoon clattered against the side of her bowl. For a moment, she felt hot and disoriented, and it felt as though the walls of the dining room were closing in on her. Her entire body was shaking. She was certain that if she tried to stand, her legs would crumble beneath her.

"But…" she faded out. Nothing made sense. Why would her mother abandon her at the gates of the workhouse, only to reappear seventeen years later? This was some kind of joke. It had to be.

She stared at Lady Caroline, unsure of what to do. A part of her wanted to rush from the hotel and never see the woman she now realised was her mother again. Another part of her wanted to fly into her arms. Most of all, she needed answers to the chaos of questions that were racing through her head.

"You're my mother?" she said, testing the words.

Lady Caroline nodded, tears dropping from her chin and landing in the dark green folds of her skirts. "Yes."

Beth's throat tightened. None of this felt real. She had given up the dream of finding her mother years ago. Had managed to put it from her mind. She had made peace with the fact that she would never know her parents, just as Mrs Whitaker had urged her to do.

And yet now here she was, sitting across from a woman who claimed to be her mother. How could this be happening?

A sudden swell of anger rose within her.

"Why?" she managed. "Why would you abandon me?"

Lady Caroline's tears fell harder. "I know it sounds like an excuse," she began, "but I truly had no choice." She took a lace handkerchief from her purse and wiped her eyes. She drew in her breath, trying to steady herself. "My father is the Earl of Derbyshire. He prides himself on the good standing of his family. When he discovered I was with child outside of wedlock, he had me sent to Bethlem Asylum – the Bedlam. Told them the pressure of becoming an unmarried mother had driven me mad."

She wrung the handkerchief between her hands.

"I wanted nothing more than to keep you," she said. "I didn't care if I had to do it without my family. I didn't care how I would manage it. The only thing that mattered was you.

"But on the day you were born they took you from my arms. I tried to fight but it was no use."

Beth felt her own tears welling. She reached out suddenly and grasped Lady Caroline's hand, her anger disappearing. She squeezed her mother's hand tightly.

"I'm sorry," Lady Caroline coughed. "I'm so terribly sorry I wasn't stronger for you. I'm so terribly sorry you've been through all you have."

Beth smiled through her tears. "You've nothing to be sorry for. Truly. It was not your fault." She looked into her mother's eyes. The same dark eyes as hers, Beth realised with a jolt. How had she never noticed that before?

"I've had a fortunate life," she said gently. "I was lucky enough to be apprenticed from the workhouse. And when she was alive, Mr Whitaker's wife was so very kind to me. She made me feel so loved."

Lady Caroline smiled. "I'm so glad of it." She laced her fingers through Beth's. "I always imagined seeing you again. I spent seventeen years wondering who you were and how your life had turned out. Whenever I passed young girls in the street, I would look at them, hoping one might be you."

Beth let her tears fall freely. "When I was a little girl in the workhouse, I used to imagine you would come and collect me. I told myself stories about who you might be."

"How I wish I could have done that, Beth," coughed Lady Caroline. "I wish it more than you could know. I spent so many years searching for you, hoping for the very same eventuality."

"How did you find me?" Beth asked. "How did you know I was working for Mr Whitaker?"

"I hired a man to investigate." Lady Caroline told her. "He found out you had been taken to Southwark Workhouse. The moment I found out, I went to the workhouse. I paid the master well to tell me who you had been apprenticed to. And then I went to Mr Whitaker's shop at once. I prayed you were still there." She smiled, squeezing Beth's fingers. "I couldn't believe it when I saw you there behind the counter. The moment I saw you, I knew exactly who you were."

"Why didn't you tell me who you were on that day?" Beth asked shakily.

"I wanted to," Lady Caroline admitted. "I wanted to tell you everything at once. But I knew it would come as a shock to you. I thought perhaps it would be easier for you if you got to know me a little first." She lowered her eyes. "And perhaps a part of me was also afraid. I was afraid you might think I had abandoned you. I was afraid you might turn me away. And I couldn't bear that."

Beth lurched suddenly out of her chair and threw her arms around her mother. She squeezed tightly, burying her head in Lady Caroline's shoulder. How long she had been dreaming of this very moment. She clung tightly to Lady Caroline, a part of her terrified she might suddenly disappear.

Lady Caroline pressed her hand to Beth's cheek. "You have no idea how long I've been wanting to hold you like that."

"I do," said Beth. "I've wanted that too. For years, I longed for nothing else." She sat back in her chair, her mother's hand between both of hers. "And my father?" she asked finally. "Who was he?"

Lady Caroline looked down. "Oh, Beth. Your father... He was a gentleman of the nobility. I was young and foolish. Younger than you are now. I thought we were in love. I was convinced we would one day marry. But when I told him I was with child, I never heard from him again." She wiped her eyes. "I'm so sorry."

Beth managed a smile. She shook her head. "You've nothing to be sorry for." It didn't matter that her father had disappeared, she realised. It didn't matter at all. Because for the first time in her life, she had a mother. The day she had longed for – and had never truly believed would materialise – had finally come.

She thought back to the stories she had told herself about her mother when she still lived in the workhouse. Thought of all the tales she and the other children had concocted about their origins and the reasons behind their abandonment.

My papa lives in a big house with lots of servants in it. And he's trying to hunt me down so he can take me back there.

My mama works for the queen. In the palace and everything.

But for all her daydreams and stories, Beth had never imagined this. Both her parents were of the aristocracy. All the while Beth had been peeling potatoes at the workhouse, she'd had noble blood coursing through her veins.

Bewildered, Beth glanced about her at the lavish decor of the hotel. How different her life might have been. All this time she had been stitching gowns for London's ladies while she had descended from their world.

The thought left an odd unsteadiness inside her as though the earth she had walked on for the past seventeen years was about to give way beneath her.

But then she realised that, in a strange sort of way, she felt just the same as she always had. She was still Beth Thursday. Still an apprentice to Mr Whitaker, still a former workhouse orphan. Only now she had a mother.

Lady Caroline glanced across the room and her eyes widened suddenly. She dropped her teacup in its saucer, making it clatter loudly.

Beth followed her gaze to see three men in dark suits striding towards them.

Lady Caroline got hurriedly to her feet. She grabbed Beth's arm. "We need to leave," she said sharply. "Now."

They began to walk briskly across the dining room, weaving through tables and heading for the stairs at the back of the room.

Beth glanced over her shoulder. The men quickened their pace, gaining on them. One clattered into a table as he passed, knocking over a teacup and eliciting a gasp from the lady at the table.

Before she could make sense of it, the three men were upon them. They shoved Beth out of the way and grabbed Lady Caroline in a vice-like grip. "Let go of me!" she hissed.

"Who are you?" Beth demanded. "What do you want?" She watched in horror as the men began to drag her mother across the room. Lady Caroline struggled against them, but they wrenched her arms behind her back.

"Please!" Beth cried. "Let her go!"

The men kept shoving Lady Caroline towards the door, as though they had not even heard her.

Beth whirled around, clutching at the arm of one of the waiters in the hotel. "Please, sir! You have to help her!"

The waiter glanced in horror at the footmen, then turned away.

"These are my father's men, Beth!" Lady Caroline cried as they dragged her to the door. "He'll do anything to stop me from finding you! He'll do anything to stop you and me from being together!"

"Quiet," hissed one of the footmen, shoving her out the door.

Beth raced out into the street. She watched helplessly as two of the men shoved Lady Caroline into the carriage and slammed the door.

The third man strode up to Beth, standing in front of her to block her view of the coach. "I apologise," he said evenly. "Lady Caroline has a long history of madness. She should not have been permitted out on her own like this and I apologise for any lies she may have told you. I hope she has not harmed you in any way."

Beth said nothing, her lips parted and her heart knocking against her ribs. Sensing he was to get no response, the footman strode back the coach and climbed into the box seat. Beth stared wide-eyed as the carriage turned the corner and disappeared.

CHAPTER 14

*B*eth stumbled down the street, trailing a hand along the buildings she passed in an attempt to keep her balance. She felt trapped in a nightmare.

But this was no dream, she knew. Lady Caroline, her mother, was in trouble and Beth had to help her. She had no idea where to even begin. Had no idea even in which direction the coach had gone.

She closed her eyes to steady herself against the chaos that had unfolded. A dull headache had formed behind her eyes.

What was she to do? Where was she to go?

After hovering on the corner for several minutes, Beth decided she had little choice but to return home.

She could hardly wander the streets all night searching for her mother. Besides, Mr Whitaker would likely awaken soon and demand his supper. Beth knew she would face endless questioning if she was not there.

She began to walk, before realising she had lost her bearings. Which way was the hotel? Which way was home? In her overwhelmed state, Beth had become completely disoriented. She blinked hard, trying to focus.

She approached an older woman who was walking hand in hand with a young boy. "Excuse me," she coughed. "Can you tell me how to get back to Kensington?"

"Kensington?" the woman repeated. "You're a way out of your way, my dear."

Beth nodded distractedly and began to walk in the direction the woman had pointed. Her thoughts were racing. Had Lady Caroline been honest with her? Had she truly been forced into giving up her child? Or was the Earl of Derbyshire's footman telling the truth? Was the woman inflicted with madness?

Lady Caroline had always seemed a little flighty, but Beth had never had a sense that she was unstable. And then there was the undeniable physical resemblance. Looking into Lady Caroline's eyes was like looking into a mirror.

Those men were lying, Beth was certain. They had to be.

But by the time she had made it back to the shop, Beth's certainty was beginning to waver. She had spent her entire life dreaming of her mother, had imagined meeting her so many times. Was it possible she was seeing something that simply was not there? Had her desperation for a mother blinded her to the truth?

Beth let herself into the shop and began to pace, her shoes clicking rhythmically against the floorboards. The sound of it helped to steady her thoughts a little. Southwark Workhouse, Lady Caroline had said. Was that where Mr Whitaker had found her? Beth had never thought to ask.

She had always thought of the place as simply *The Workhouse*, but now she considered the matter, Beth realised there were many such places in London.

She trudged upstairs and peeked into the parlour.

Mr Whitaker looked up. "I was calling you," he barked. "Why did you not come?"

"I'm sorry, Mr Whitaker. I was down in the storeroom," she lied. "I'm afraid I didn't hear you."

Mr Whitaker snorted in response.

"Would you like some supper?" Beth asked.

Mr Whitaker sat up, rubbing his red eyes. His cheeks were flushed pink, the rest of his face pale. His grey beard had grown long and patchy. "Supper," he coughed. "Yes. Fetch me some supper. I'm famished. And none of that watery rubbish you served up yesterday."

Obediently, Beth went to the kitchen. The remains of last night's watery stew were still sitting on the range. Beth went to the cold room for the meat she had bought the day before. She added a little more to the stew, along with a good helping of spices. Mr Whitaker would be more amenable to her questions, Beth knew, if she fed him satisfactorily.

She went back to his bedroom and handed him a steaming bowl. "Be careful," she warned. "It's hot."

Mr Whitaker grunted in response. He lay back on his pillow, the bowl pressed to his chest.

Beth hovered in the doorway, watching him lift the spoon to his mouth. Stew drizzled down his chin.

"What do you want?" he grunted. "Why are you standing there like a fool?"

"Southwark Workhouse," Beth blurted. "Was that where you found me?"

Mr Whitaker's nose wrinkled. "Why do you want to know that?"

"No reason," Beth said quickly. "Please, sir. Just tell me. Was it Southwark Workhouse?"

Mr Whitaker stirred his soup, bringing a chunk of meat to his mouth. "Aye," he said finally, his mouth full. "Southwark Workhouse. That's right."

CHAPTER 15

*B*eth lay awake long into the night. Her mind was racing. She churned through every second of her conversation with Lady Caroline, remembering the words she had spent her life longing to hear.

I'm your mother, Beth.

And then she thought of those terrifying men in black who had forced Lady Caroline into the carriage. Where had they taken her? What were they doing to her? The thought made Beth's stomach tighten.

And despite herself, she couldn't help the footman's words from circling through her mind.

Lady Caroline has a long history of madness. I apologise for any lies she may have told you.

No. Lady Caroline had not told her lies. Beth was sure of it.

Wasn't she?

Southwark Workhouse. Had it been just a lucky guess on Lady Caroline's part? Or had she truly hired a thief-taker to hunt down her daughter? Had she truly paid the workhouse master to give her the information she had craved? Information on the infant daughter that had been forced from her arms at birth?

IN THE MORNING, Beth made her way to the library.

"I believe there's a book," she said uncertainly, "on the nobility. I..." She twisted her fingers together edgily. "It lists people?"

The librarian nodded, poking his glasses back up his nose. "Yes," he said. "Of course. *Debrett's*. I'll find you a copy. This way."

Beth nodded her thanks. The librarian led her across the room towards the shelves. He peered at the rows of books, scratching his shorn chin.

"Ah," he said finally. "Here we are. *Debrett's Peerage and Baronetage.*" He slid the large, leather-bound book from the shelf and placed it in Beth's arms. "This one almost five years old," he told her.

Beth gave a small smile. "This will do just fine. Thank you."

She carried the book to a table in the corner of the library. She ran her fingers over the elaborately decorated cover and opened the volume carefully.

She began to leaf through the pages, searching for information on the Earl of Derbyshire. The words swam in front of Beth's weary, sleep-deprived eyes. She blinked hard, trying to focus.

Her fingers glided down the page and stopped as she found the name. William Speers, seventh Earl of Derbyshire. Five children. Among them, Lady Caroline Speers.

Beth let out her breath and leant back in her chair. Lady Caroline had been telling the truth about her father. Had she been telling the truth about her daughter too?

Somewhere deep inside, Beth knew she had been. She had felt a connection to Lady Caroline the moment she had stepped inside the shop. A connection that went far deeper than their shared brown eyes and dark curls. A connection she had not been able to articulate until now.

Had Lady Caroline also been telling the truth when she had claimed the men in black were the

Earl's men, desperate to keep mother and daughter apart?

Beth rubbed her eyes. The thought of it made the anger bubble inside her.

Regardless of the information she had learned, she felt helpless. Regardless of whose blood was coursing through her, the world saw her as no more than a lowly seamstress. A workhouse orphan. What business did she have getting involved in the issues of the nobility?

Beth shook the thought away angrily. She had every right, she told herself. Lady Caroline was her mother. The woman she had spent her whole life longing for. She had to help her.

Beth reached into her pocket and pulled out Lady Caroline's calling card.

If Mr Whitaker causes you trouble... or if there is anything else you need, you may find me at this address.

Beth shoved the book back onto the shelf and hurried out of the library.

SHE STOOD for a long time staring up at the townhouse. Three storeys loomed above her, each painted in white and adorned with wide windows.

Chimneys dotted the red-tiled roof and a wide garden stretched out in front of the building. Mr and Mrs Whitaker's comfortable lodgings about the shop felt like a hovel compared to this.

This was her family's home, Beth told herself. Never mind the fact that her family wanted nothing to do with her. This was the world she had been born out of, if not into.

Beth fixed her gaze on the front door. She ought to knock. But what would she say? She knew well enough that the Earl of Derbyshire would deny all knowledge of her. Would deny Lady Caroline's story.

Lady Caroline was clearly being punished for having sought out her illegitimate child in the first place. How could things possibly be made better by that child revealing herself?

No, Beth decided. If she was to show her face on the Earl's doorstep, it would make matters endlessly worse for her mother. She wanted desperately to help but knew within herself that this was not the way. With a sinking feeling in her chest, she turned away from the house and trudged back towards the tailor's shop.

* * *

When Beth arrived at the shop, two well-dressed men were waiting outside. The sight of them made Beth's heart quicken. In their dark suits and tightly knotted cravats, they reminded her very much of the men who had forced Lady Caroline into the carriage.

"Can I help you?" she asked.

"We're looking for Mr James Whitaker," said one of the men. Beth swallowed heavily. She knew Mr Whitaker was likely passed out in his bed, sleeping off the previous night's excesses.

"Mr Whitaker is unavailable at the moment," she said shortly.

The men eyed each other.

"You work here?" asked one.

"Yes, sir. I'm Mr Whitaker's apprentice."

"Perhaps we might speak inside?"

Beth nodded stiffly and pulled a key from her pocket. She slid it into the lock and let the two men into the shop.

"I'm afraid we are acting on the order of the courts," said the first man. "Your employer, Mr Whitaker is to be taken to debtors' prison." He held out the documents in his grasp.

Beth felt suddenly cold. "What?" she managed. "Debtor's prison?" She tried to scan the pages. The words seemed to blur in front of her eyes. Mr Whitaker couldn't go to prison. For all his flaws, Beth had no thought of how she might manage without him. With Mr Whitaker gone, what would become of his shop? What would become of her?

She felt a sudden sense of failure. Mrs Whitaker had raised her to take care of the family shop. She had raised her in place of the daughter she had never had. And here it was about to fall into the hands of the debtors. Beth forced herself to breathe, gripping the edge of the counter to steady herself.

"Is Mr Whitaker on the premises?" asked one of the men.

Beth closed her eyes. "Yes," she admitted. "He's upstairs."

She watched as they disappeared up the stairs. Ought she to follow them, Beth wondered? Ought she to try to offer Mr Whitaker some reassurance to that he was not alone?

She sighed in frustration. What assurance could she give? She had no way of helping Mr Whitaker. And she knew in all likelihood he would want nothing to do with her anyway.

She could hear the men's muffled voices coming from upstairs. An angry cry from Mr Whitaker. Beth's stomach lurched.

And then the footsteps were coming back towards the stairs. The men reappeared, herding Mr Whitaker down into the shop. He was walking dizzily, clattering into the handrail, hissing and cursing under his breath.

His eyes fell to Beth and he looked at her pleadingly. "Do you see this, Elizabeth?" he demanded. "Stop this! Do something, would you!"

Beth looked down. "I'm sorry, sir. There's nothing I can do."

"The girl is right," one of the men told Mr Whitaker with a hint of a smile. "You've brought all this on yourself. It doesn't take a wise man to see where all your money has gone."

Mr Whitaker narrowed his eyes and cursed at the men.

One of them clamped Mr Whitaker's arms behind his back while the other marched into the storeroom.

"What are you doing?" Beth demanded.

"We're under orders to take anything of value," he told her, scooping up the reams of satin Beth had purchased to make Lady Caroline's gowns. Beth stared despairingly at the empty shelves.

"What will happen to the shop?" she asked. "And the house?"

"I'm afraid they will likely be sold to cover the debt," said the first man. Beth could see pity in his eyes. He looked back over his shoulder at her as they marched Mr Whitaker towards the door. "I suggest you begin looking for somewhere else to live."

CHAPTER 16

Beth lay in bed staring at the ceiling. With Mr Whitaker gone, the house felt cold and empty. How could she feel his absence so acutely, she wondered, when they had barely spoken more than a few words to each other in years? She shivered, pulling her blanket tightly around her. She longed to light the fire, but how could she waste money on coal? She had no idea when the debtors would reappear and take the house and the shop. Had no idea how long it would be before she was flung out on the street with nowhere to go and no one to turn to.

No, Beth realised. She didn't have no one. After seventeen years of hoping and praying, she had finally found her mother. And right now, both she and Lady Caroline needed each other.

EARLY THE NEXT MORNING, Beth stood outside the vast expanse of the Earl of Derbyshire's house. She felt gripped by the same anxiety she had felt the last time she was here. She wrestled it away. What choice did she have but to knock? Lady Caroline was the only hope she had. Without her, Beth knew there was every chance she would end up back at the workhouse.

Her presence here would make things worse for her mother, Beth knew. But what was the alternative? And while she had little experience in being someone's daughter, she knew in her heart her mother would do everything she could to help her.

Even if that meant facing the wrath of the Earl.

Sucking in her breath, Beth marched up the stairs and knocked on the huge black door of the house Her heart raced. She heard rhythmic footsteps approaching, then the door was pulled open and a tall, dour-faced butler was peering down at her.

"Yes?"

Beth cleared her throat. "I wish to see Lady Caroline," she said as loudly and clearly as she could manage.

The butler eyed her. "And you are?"

Beth hesitated. "Just a friend."

The butler pressed his lips into a thin white line. "May I have your calling card?"

"My calling card?" Beth stammered. "I... uh... I'm afraid I don't have one." She felt the colour rising in her cheeks and cursed herself. No one would believe a woman like Lady Caroline would have a friend who didn't have a calling card. Surely the butler would send her away. Tell her never to return.

But instead, he sighed heavily and gestured for Beth to enter. "Wait here," he told her, disappearing into the vast passages of the house.

Beth looked around in disbelief. The lavishness of Lady Caroline's carriage was nothing compared to this. Lord Derbyshire's manor house felt like a palace, with its high white ceilings and elaborate gold cornices. A wide staircase rose up from the entrance hall, the steps dark polished wood.

Beth's gaze fell to a large family portrait hanging in the stairwell. A man and woman Beth guessed to be the Earl and Countess of Derbyshire were seated at the centre, a large brood of well-dressed children surrounding them.

Beth's eyes fixed on a young girl to the left of her father. She wore a navy-blue gown, long dark curls falling over her shoulders and large brown eyes staring straight ahead. Beth exhaled sharply. She could have been looking at a portrait of herself. She stared at the portrait for a long time, feeling any last shreds of doubt falling away.

Footsteps sounded back down the hall, drawing her out of her thoughts. Instead of the butler, an older man was approaching. Beth recognised him as the man who had spoken to her outside the hotel. He had been one of the men who had forced Lady Caroline into the carriage. Beth felt the back of her neck prickle with anger.

He looked her up and down, scrutinising. Beth pressed her shoulders back indignantly, her eyes meeting his. Her nerves, she realised, had been replaced with anger.

"I'm very sorry, miss," he said, in the same even voice he had used at the hotel, "but I'm afraid Lady Caroline is not in residence at present."

"What do you mean she's not in residence?" Beth said sharply. "Where is she?"

The footman bristled. "That's no business of yours, Miss…"

"Elizabeth Thursday," said Beth, meeting the man's eyes with a firm stare.

And it is my business, she wanted to say. *What happens to my mother is very much my business...*

Instead, she said: "When is she expected back?"

"Not for some time, I'm afraid."

"Where is she?" Beth asked again.

The footman sighed. "Must I repeat myself, Miss Thursday? Lady Caroline's movements have nothing to do with you, as I suspect you well know."

Beth clenched her jaw. "Then I shall just have to keep calling until she has returned," she said.

The footman pressed his lips into a thin smile. "About that, Miss Thursday..." He reached into his pocket and produced a small coin pouch. "Compliments of the Earl of Derbyshire." He pressed his lips into a thin white line. "In exchange for your never calling here again."

Beth looked down at the pouch in disbelief. Was the Earl really trying to buy her silence? Did he truly believe a few miserable coins would be enough to persuade her to turn her back on her long-yearned for mother?

A part of her longed to fling those coins back in the footman's face. But she was in no position to turn down money. She snatched the pouch and shoved it into her pocket. Stormed out of the house without another word.

CHAPTER 17

Beth marched back to the shop in a rage. The audacity of the Earl! How dare he treat her in such a way! Illegitimate child or not, she was his *granddaughter!* Though Beth had never truly had a family of her own, she imagined that such a thing might warrant a little more loyalty.

She squeezed her hand around the pouch in her pocket, desperately wishing she had been in a position to turn it down.

In her anger, she had almost forgotten her impending eviction.

But when she arrived back at the shop, the notice on the door yanked her back to reality. She snatched the page and scanned over it, the sick feeling in her stomach intensifying.

The shop was to be taken back into ownership by the bank at the end of the month.

Beth closed her eyes, calculating. The end of the month was just twenty-two days from now.

Feeling suddenly exhausted, she let herself into the shop and settled behind the counter. There was little point, she knew. Lady Caroline had been her only customer in weeks. And even if, by miracle, someone was to request her services, she had no material with which to create, no buttons or thread or needles with which to mend. The men in black had taken everything.

She pulled a chair out from the storeroom and sank into it, looking out over the bare walls of the shop. She had been so full of optimism when she had first started to work here. She thought of learning to embroider with Mrs Whitaker. Thought of the sense of pride she had felt when she had stitched her first gowns. And now? In a few weeks, she would have nothing.

Her home would be gone, her livelihood gone.

Her mother, gone.

She closed her eyes wearily. Somewhere in the back of her mind, she realised, she was waiting for the bell above the door to ring. Waiting for her mother to come floating through the door to save her. Just as she had done in her days at the workhouse.

The ache of losing Lady Caroline was fierce. Beth had gone her whole life without a mother, but it was nothing compared to the loneliness she felt now. How could she have found her mother at last, only to have her so cruelly taken away?

And never mind the ache in her chest, Beth had to focus on her own survival. Without her tools and fabrics, she had no way of earning a living. Where would she go at the end of the month when the bank reclaimed the house? What would she do?

Her finely stitched dresses would earn her a few shillings, she decided. Enough to pay for fresh needles and thread. Enough to keep her working for a few more weeks at least.

Resolutely, Beth climbed upstairs to her bedroom. She took the gowns from her wardrobe and laid them carefully on her bed. Five gowns, all neatly stitched and embroidered. The thought of parting with them filled her with sadness. But what choice did she have?

She folded them neatly, ready to be taken to the market. She would survive, Beth told herself. She always survived. It was in her very makeup. But right now, she wanted nothing more than to curl up in a ball and hide from the world. She had never felt more alone in her life.

* * *

AT THE END of the month, Beth bundled up her few remaining belongings and bid an agonising farewell to the house that had been her home for the past nine years. She moved silently from room to room, trying to commit the lodgings to her memory.

What joy she had felt when Mrs Whitaker had first led her to her bedroom as an eight-year-old girl. How excited she had been at the thought of having a bed all of her own.

She stood in the doorway of the parlour, remembering the evenings she and Mrs Whitaker had spent in front of the fire. Remembering how, for the first time in her life, she had felt cared for. Loved.

But now the room, like the rest of the house, felt cold and hollow. The stale tang of Mr Whitaker's brandy hung in the air, the empty grate a reminder of how many nights they had shivered and struggled. Any good memories she had had of this place were gone, Beth realised. They had died with Mrs Whitaker.

She lifted the floorboard and removed her

savings. She swung her bag onto her shoulder and made her way downstairs. Stepped out of the house without looking back.

BETH HEADED EAST, her fist clutched around the pouch of coins in her pocket. For three weeks, she had eaten barely a thing, and lit no fire, saving every penny so she might keep a roof over her head. She would find a room in a tenement, she told herself or failing that, a bed in a lodging house. And she would find work. After all, she had fine skills. Even Mr Whitaker had told her as much.

She found a room in a dark and creaking tenement on the outskirts of Whitechapel. The space was cramped and cold; the single window patched with a dirty brown cloth. There was no fireplace, and the bed was little more than a scrap of blanket on the floor. Still, Beth told herself, it was shelter. And that was something.

Her stomach groaning, and she bought a loaf of bread and sat on the blanket to eat it. She chewed slowly, savouring the feel of food on her tongue. She could hear every word of the conversation in the room beside hers; two women arguing over who owned a blanket, while a baby wailed over the top of them.

For a moment, Beth was back in the workhouse, listening to the chatter and cries of the children crammed in around her.

She had made her way out of the workhouse, she reminded herself. And she would get out of this place too. She would find Lady Caroline and the two of them would start again. After all, as lonely as Beth felt as she listened to the bickering of the women in the next room, she had a mother now. Wherever Lady Caroline was, whatever was happening to her, she knew Beth was alive. And that was what she had to cling to.

IN THE MORNING, Beth set out to buy the newspaper, desperate to find herself a new job before her money ran out. *You've a talent with a needle and thread, and you've a talent with people,* Mrs Whitaker had told her the night before she had died. *Those things are going to get you far in life. I've never been more sure of anything.*

Yes, thought Beth. She had to remember that. She couldn't lose hope. Mr and Mrs Whitaker had trained her well, and she had kept the shop running for years almost single-handedly. Surely she could find enough work to keep a roof over her head.

She took the newspaper back to her tenement and hunched on the floor to read it. The pages were full of job openings for cooks and gardeners, housemaids and governesses. Little work for a seamstress.

Perhaps she could find work as a maid, Beth reasoned. After all, she had held the household together after Mrs Whitaker's death. Still, Beth knew such a thing was unlikely to count for experience in the eyes of an employer.

Finally, she stumbled upon a small advertisement at the bottom of the page.

Seamstress wanted for slop work. Regular pay.

Beth had always considered herself lucky not to be engaged in slop work – the production of ready-to-wear pieces for the ever-growing middle class. Mr and Mrs Whitaker had been wildly against the practice, adamant that their shop produced only the highest quality custom-made clothing.

But this was no time to be selective. Beth knew well that any woman with a leaky tenement roof over her head would be a fool to turn down any kind of work, no matter how low quality and poorly paid.

She began to scrawl a hurried letter of application.

***

Within the week, Beth found herself engrossed in slop work, hired to make a seemingly endless number of men's shirts and women's shifts. She worked in the draughty silence of her room in the tenement, hunched on the floor in the centre of the room, stitching until her candle flame hissed and spat and disappeared.

Each day was long and monotonous as she churned out piece after identical piece. Her fingers ached constantly, and her eyes strained as she attempted to sew by the dim candlelight. Still, she reminded herself as she collapsed onto her thin sleeping pallet each night, it was work. And it was keeping her off the street.

But as the weeks wore on, Beth began to realise that the pay she was receiving for the slop work would barely cover her rent. Most days, she ate little more than a few mouthfuls of bread. She knew it would not be long before she could no longer keep a roof over her head.

What was she to do? There was no option of taking on more work – she already spent every waking hour sewing. There was simply no more time in the day. Despite Mrs Whitaker's confidence that Beth's skills would get her far in life, she was beginning to see that simply was not the case. Her only option was to find another, better-paid position, and an employer who would see past her lack of experience.

Beth found herself poring over the job pages of the newspaper again. *Nursery maid, stable hand, housekeeper...* All positions for which she was wildly unqualified. She kept scanning the page. *Scullery maid.*

Perhaps she could manage such a thing.

The next morning, Beth set out for the townhouse in Lambeth that had advertised the position. She wore the blue woollen gown she had stitched herself; the only one of her dresses she had not sold at the market.

After weeks living on little but stale bread, the dress hung loosely from her body. Beth glanced at her reflection in the cracked window of the tenement. Her once rosy cheeks had become sallow and thin, her curls hanging limply around her face. The sight of herself made her heart ache. She had not realised what a miserable effect these past weeks had had on her body.

She turned away from the window and went to the washbowl in the corner of the room. A thin layer of ice glistened on the surface. Beth dipped her hands into the thin puddle of water. She splashed her face, gasping at the coldness. Perhaps the icy water would bring a little colour back to her pale cheeks. She combed her hair and wrangled it into a plait which she then pinned it neatly at her neck. Then she used the remaining water from the basin to scrub the mud from her boots.

She considered taking in the seams of the ill-fitting dress. Would such a thing take up too much time?

In the end, she pulled the dress over her head and sat in the centre of the room, drawing in the seams of the bodice. It would be time well-spent, she told herself as her needle flew in and out of the soft fabric. She would be far better dressed when she made it to her would-be employer's house.

She slipped the dress back on and stood before the window to take in her reflection. A definite improvement, she decided. With her combed hair and altered dress, she looked almost presentable.

She slid on her cloak and set out for the house in Lambeth. The walk across town would be a long one, and Beth couldn't help but think of all the sewing work she would be missing out on that day. If she did not get this job as a scullery maid, she would have to work all night tonight just to scrape together enough for her rent.

She *would* get the job, she told herself. She was well-presented and well-spoken and hard-working. Everything a potential employer could hope for.

It was late afternoon by the time she reached the employer's townhouse. Beth began to regret altering her dress. Perhaps she had wasted precious time.

She strode up to the front door and knocked loudly.

Footsteps sounded down the hall, and for a moment Beth was back outside the Derbyshire's Townhouse, her heart racing as she waited to confront the Earl. She smoothed her skirts and tried to focus.

A maid in a cloth cap opened the door. "Yes?"

Beth cleared her throat. "I'm here about the scullery maid position."

The woman scratched her chin, clearly bored. "Position was filled this morning, I'm afraid."

"I see." Beth forced a smile. "I'm sorry to have bothered you."

She trudged back down the stairs, a sinking

feeling in her chest. What had she been thinking, wasting precious time mending her dress?

She began to trudge back towards Whitechapel. Already her legs were aching, and her stomach groaned with hunger. She would buy herself a little bread on the way home, she told herself, then she would return to the tenement and begin her slop work.

She shivered as a cold wind blew her hair from her cheeks. She wrapped her arms around herself to keep out the chill. She could feel dampness soaking through a hole in the bottom of her shoe.

Noble blood, she thought, laughing humourlessly to herself. *Noble blood, and still it has come to this.*

A sudden shout behind her yanked Beth from her thoughts.

She spun around to find a carriage tearing down the road towards her. Beth flung herself out of the coach's path, landing heavily on her knees in the mud on the edge of the road. The coachman cursed at her, then snapped the reins, goading his horses forward.

Beth gulped down her breath, trying to steady her racing heart. She had not even realised she had drifted out into the middle of the road. She climbed shakily to her feet, brushing the mud from her skirts. And then she stopped.

The carriage had come to a halt not far down the street. A well-dressed man and woman were climbing out. They had a vague familiarity to them.

Keeping to the dusky shadows, Beth hurried towards them. As their faces became clearer, Beth felt a bolt of shock. She had seen this couple in the portrait hanging in the stairwell at the Earl's townhouse.

The carriage that had almost run her down belonged to Lord Derbyshire.

Beth stood for a moment with her back pressed to the wall, trying to decide what to do. The Earl had not deliberately tried to run her down; of that she was certain. After all, how would he have known where to find her? But it didn't change the fact that he had tried to buy her silence. And he had done something terrible to her mother, Beth knew it without a doubt.

Beth watched as the Earl and Countess disappeared into a dimly lit building on the corner of the street. She peered through the window. The room was decorated with crimson curtains, a fire raging in an enormous black grate. A large polished wood bar stretched from one end of the room to the other, while well-dressed men and women sashayed about with glasses in their hands.

Beth squinted. Some kind of private club, she guessed. She watched as Lady Derbyshire greeted two ladies with a kiss on the cheek.

Beth glanced at the broad-shouldered doorman. He was dressed in a long black greatcoat, his arms folded behind his back. His eyes darted from side to side, watching as figures strode up and down the street.

There was no way he would let her in, of course. Even with her cleaned boots and altered dress, she still looked as though she had crawled out of the Whitechapel tenements. She stayed hidden in the shadows, watching the building closely.

Perhaps there was a back entrance or a window she could climb through. Either way, she had to seize this chance. Had to find out what the Earl had done to her mother.

After she had stood waiting for what felt like hours, Beth was startled by shouting. Two men stumbled out of a tavern a few doors down from the club and charged across the street, hurling abuse at one another. Beth pressed her back hard against the wall, trying to disappear. One of the men swung a wild punch, striking the other on the chin. He stumbled to his knees, before hurling a fierce blow of his own. The doorman hurried into the street, shouting at the two men.

Beth seized her chance. She darted through the door of the club.

Inside it was hot, the fire blazing in an enormous grate, with lamps dotted along the walls. Laughter and voices mingled with the clink of glasses. Beth hugged her shawl around her tightly, feeling immensely out of place. She peered edgily through the crowd in search of the Earl.

Everyone was well-dressed, in neatly tailored coats and wide, flounced gowns. In the dim light, it was difficult to make out faces.

"You all right there, miss?" a brassy voice behind her made Beth jump. She whirled around to see an older man with a glass of liquor in his hand. He leered down at her, his cheeks pink with the drink. He smelled of whisky and sweat. He chuckled. "You look a little lost."

"No," she said tautly. "I'm quite all right. I—" She stopped abruptly, picking out the figure of the Earl in the corner of the room. At the sight of him, all her nerves evaporated. All she felt was anger and determination. She strode away from the drunkard without looking back, pushing past the other patrons to reach the Earl.

She fixed him with fierce eyes. She was determined for him to acknowledge her. Determined for him to tell her Lady Caroline whereabouts. She was not leaving here until she found her mother.

"Lord Derbyshire."

The Earl and his wife turned in surprise. Up close, Beth could see the Countess had the same dark brown eyes as she and Lady Caroline.

The Earl glanced down at Beth as though she was a dog that had slunk in through the back door. "Who are you?" he asked disdainfully. "And how in heaven's name did you get in here?"

She looked at him squarely. "I'm your granddaughter," she said. "And I want to know what you've done with my mother."

The Earl's eyes widened, colour rushing to his cheeks. The Countess's eyes darted between her husband and Beth. She tossed back the remains of the wine in her glass.

"I don't know what in God's name you're talking about, girl," the Earl hissed. "All I know is you've no right being in a place such as this."

Beth's stare didn't falter. "You know exactly what

I'm talking about," she said icily. "You tried to buy my silence, but it won't work." She turned to the Countess. "Are you in on this too? Where is Lady Caroline?"

The Countess turned away hurriedly.

Lord Derbyshire stared down at Beth. "Get out of here," he hissed. "I don't ever want to see you again. You have no place in our lives."

Beth stared him down. She realised conversations around them had stopped. Everyone in the club was staring at her and the Earl. She pressed her shoulders back and lifted her chin. "I'm not going anywhere until you tell me what you've done with my mother."

The Earl raised a hand and clicked his fingers. His men, dressed in their customary black suits, strode towards him. One glanced at Beth with recognition in his eyes.

"Her again, My Lord?" he said, a hint of humour in his voice.

The Earl's eyes were dark. "Take her upstairs," he said. "Restrain her. I'll make the necessary arrangements."

"Of course, My Lord."

Beth felt suddenly hot, then cold. The men came towards her, each grabbing one arm and dragging her backwards.

"Let go of me!" she shrieked, kicking wildly. Her feet found nothing but air. One of the men grabbed her under the arms, the other pinning her ankles together. They carried her towards a dark, narrow staircase at the back of the club. Beth thrashed against her captors. She tried to shriek, but a firm hand was clamped over her mouth. Hot fear raced through her. What did the Earl mean to do to her? Surely he wouldn't kill her. Would he? What did he mean by the *necessary arrangements?*

As they reached a corridor at the top of the stairs, the man holding her ankles released her, letting her feet fall heavily to the floor. The other kept his arms firmly around her, preventing her from running away.

The footman unlocked a narrow door and shoved Beth inside. She stumbled, landing on her knees before scrambling to her feet and whirling around to face the men.

"What does he want?" she garbled. "Just let me go! Please!"

Neither spoke. They pulled the door closed with a heavy click. Beth rushed forward and rattled the door, but it was to no avail. She pounded a fist against it.

"Let me out!" she cried again. "Please!"

"Quiet!" barked one of the men.

Beth took a step back from the door and closed her eyes. She drew in a long breath, trying to slow her racing heart.

She turned in a slow circle, taking in her surroundings. The room was painted in the same dark crimson as the rest of the club. A narrow bed sat against one wall, along with an elaborately carved nightstand. Beth wrapped her arms around herself. She didn't dare imagine what this room was used for.

She went over to the window and pushed back the curtain. She was only one floor up. If she climbed out onto the roof, perhaps she could find a way down. But as she began to rattle the window, heavy footsteps sounded down the hall. The door clicked open.

Beth spun around to see the wide silhouette of the Earl. He stepped inside, his features revealing themselves in the pale lamplight.

"Don't bother," he said darkly. "The windows are locked." He folded his arms across his thick chest. "Come here," he said, narrowing his eyes.

Too afraid to do anything but obey, Beth crept across the room and peered up at him.

"Please," she squeaked. "Just let me go."

He shook his head slowly. "No. It's too late for that. You ought to have just taken the money and disappeared."

Beth felt a sudden swell of anger. "Where is Lady Caroline?" she demanded. "Where is my mother?"

The Earl's cheeks flushed pink with anger. "Lady Caroline is not your mother," he said tersely. "Lady Caroline has a history of madness, as my man told you last week. You're a fool if you have been taken in by her lies."

Beth shook her head. "They're not lies," she hissed. "I know it. And you know it too. That's why you've brought me up here."

The Earl's eyebrows shot up at her sudden sharpness. He tapped a finger against his smoothly shaved chin while he looked her up and down. He could see the similarities between herself and Lady Caroline, Beth was certain.

"Whatever my daughter has told you," he said slowly, "you are not a member of this family. You never will be. You are nothing but a workhouse orphan who has no place poking her nose into the nobility. You and those like you have no place."

Beth clenched her hands into angry fists. "I'm no orphan," she hissed. "And you know it. I'm your granddaughter."

The Earl sucked in his breath. He clicked open the door, gesturing for the two footmen to enter. "Take her to the carriage," he said.

Beth stiffened as the two men came towards her again. She stumbled backwards. "Let me go!" she cried, a fresh wave of fear sweeping over her "Please!" The footmen clamped their hands around the tops of her arms, marching her towards the door. The Earl bent close to her, his nose inches from hers. His breath was hot and stale against her skin.

"Make a sound," he hissed. "And you'll be severely punished. Do you understand?"

Beth swallowed heavily, her skin prickling with cold sweat. She managed a nod.

"Good."

The Earl strode down the stairs ahead of the footmen, disappearing into the shadows of the club.

CHAPTER 18

The footmen led Beth out into the street and threw open the door of a waiting carriage. They shoved her inside, then climbed in after her. As she stumbled onto the bench seats, Beth realised it was the same elaborately decorated carriage she had ridden to Brown's Hotel in, with its red velvet curtains and elaborately painted ceiling.

This time it was not Lady Caroline with whom she was sharing the coach, but the steely-faced Earl and his men. Lord Derbyshire sat opposite Beth, pinning her with dark, unforgiving eyes.

He rapped on the wall of the carriage, signalling to his coachman to leave.

The carriage began to rattle down the road.

"Where are we going?" Beth coughed, her voice

rattling. "Where are you taking me?" She tried to peer through the window, but one of the footmen clamped his hands over her wrists, tugging her down sharply.

"Sit still," he hissed, "or we'll have to restrain you."

"You can't do this."

"Of course, I can," he laughed. "I have money and status. You have nothing. You are nothing. I can, and I will, do as I like."

Beth gulped down air and tried to think clearly. Wherever she was being taken, she needed to have her wits about her. She closed her eyes, trying to stop the violent thundering of her heart.

After what felt like an eternity, the coach slowed to a halt. The Earl threw open the door and leapt out of the carriage, gesturing for his footmen to follow.

Beth looked around her, bewildered. She was standing among vast manicured gardens, thick with shadows in the late evening. Ahead of her was a palatial brick building, dotted with narrow windows. The whole place had a strange air of foreboding.

"What is this place?" she cried frantically. "Where are you taking me?" The footmen clamped their hands around her arms again and marched her forward.

Beth's eyes fell to the sign above the door.

Bethlem Royal Hospital.

Her stomach rolled. She had been born in this place. This was where the Earl had incarcerated Lady Caroline when she had discovered herself with child.

The Bedlam...

A wild sweep of dizziness swung over her. "You can't do this," she said. "You can't. I—"

"Quiet," hissed the Earl. He lifted the brass knocker on the front door and pounded it loudly.

"No," Beth cried frantically. "Let me go. I'll stay away from your family, I swear it. I'll never bother you or your daughter again. Please. Just let me go."

The front door creaked as it opened, revealing a young woman dressed in a shift that might have at one time been white.

"I need to see Doctor Miller," the Earl said sharply. "I have a young woman with me who must urgently be admitted."

WILLIAM SPEERS, Earl of Derbyshire, strode out of the doors of Bethlem Asylum and climbed into this waiting carriage. The back of his neck burned with anger.

Being back here brought back a flood of bad memories. Just one glimpse at the building reminded him of all the shame Caroline had brought upon his family. Shame he had thought he had managed. Eradicated. Up until recently, William Speers had been convinced he had done enough to make sure his illegitimate grandchild disappeared.

When his children were young, William had always been most fond of Caroline. She was lively, kind, clever and beautiful. He had always held out the most hope for her to make something of herself; to find the most decorated of husbands, to advance the Derbyshire name the furthest.

He had not counted on her being so foolish as to lie with a man out of wedlock. Nor had he suspected the determination that lay inside his youngest daughter.

When he had first taken Caroline to the asylum, he had assumed it the end of all their problems. The child would be born, and if it survived, it would be taken to the workhouse, never to be spoken of again.

And for years that was just how things had played out. When his eldest son's wife had given birth to a son a year later, William had celebrated it as the birth of his first grandchild, Caroline's bastard barely more than a flicker of a memory. He'd had no thought of whether it was a boy or a girl.

Of course, he had not expected Caroline to forget the child as easily as he had, but nor had he expected her to go traipsing her way around the city on a desperate search.

He had first grown suspicious when he began to notice his daughter leaving the house more often. In the years since the birth of her child – in the years since she had refused to marry – Caroline had spent much of her time at home, rarely socialising or venturing out in public.

But then she began to make strings of outings, each time leaving the house in her most elegant day wear. Each time with a determined look on her face. It made the Earl decidedly uncomfortable.

"Follow her," he told his man when he watched as Caroline left the house one day. And when the footman returned to the house later that afternoon, he brought the news the Earl had been dreading.

"She has engaged the services of an old style thief-taker," the footman reported. "I don't know for what purpose."

But William Speers knew exactly the purpose.

There was no thief to take. But their was a child to find. And it made his stomach turn over with dread.

Perhaps he was overreacting. The chances of the child surviving past infancy in the workhouse were slim at best.

Nonetheless, he was unable to still the anxiety inside him. Uncovering the existence of Caroline's child was a scandal his family could not afford.

He sent his footman out to follow her again.

"Did she go to the thief-taker again?" he demanded when the footman came to his office later that day.

"No, my lord. She merely went to the seamstress. For a new gown, perhaps."

The Earl felt the restlessness inside him begin to still. "Next time she leaves the house," he told the footman, "you will follow her again. I want to be certain I have nothing to be concerned about. If you sense anything untoward, you must let me know at once."

When the footman next came to the Earl's office, there was a frown creasing the bridge of his nose.

"What is it?" the Earl demanded, feeling decidedly uncomfortable.

"I've word from the coachman that Lady Caroline has arranged to take the young seamstress to lunch tomorrow, my lord. It seemed a rather unusual invitation. I thought it best that you know."

The following day, William Speers took a cab across London on the trail of his best carriage. He watched Caroline make her way to a tailor's shop in Kensington and collect a young woman who seemed oddly familar. He followed them to Brown's Hotel, where he sat hidden in the corner, never taking his eyes from his daughter and her companion.

William watched as Caroline and the young woman laughed, spoke, cried, embraced. And he knew, from the emotion on his daughter's face, that she had found her long lost child.

His daughter was mistaken, William tried to tell himself. The young woman opposite Caroline was not her child. The child had been disposed of at the workhouse. In all likelihood, she had not seen her first birthday. And Caroline had become as mad as the women she had found herself among during her time at Bethlem Asylum.

But William was unable to convince himself of his own ideal. He could see the striking similarity between the two women: the large dark eyes, the narrow faces, the cascades of dark curls. He felt a sick sensation in his stomach. William knew he was looking at his granddaughter.

"Remove Lady Caroline from the hotel," he instructed his men who were waiting silently behind him, waiting for orders.

"And what of the young woman?"

The Earl scratched his chin. "Lady Caroline is not of sound mind," he said tautly. "See that the young woman is made aware of that."

BUT THE YOUNG WOMAN, William soon came to realise, had the same determination as her mother. First her appearance at the townhouse, then at the club. No. It simply would not do.

I'm your granddaughter, she had told him, glaring at him with eyes so like her mother's. But she was wrong. She had no place in this family. And she needed to be made aware of that. By any means necessary.

CHAPTER 19

"Please," Beth coughed, as an attendant led her down the whitewashed corridors of the asylum. "Let me go. This is a mistake. I'm not mad, I swear it."

The attendant gave a short chuckle. "Course you're not." She unlocked one of the many doors leading off from the corridor. It opened with a creak.

With a firm hand around the top of Beth's arm, she led her into the room. It was the size of a prison cell, painted white like everything else in the building, with a narrow metal bed in the middle of the room.

The attendant held out the armful of grey

clothing she had tucked under her arm. "You're to wear this."

Beth shook her head firmly. "No," she said. "This is all a mistake. Lord Derbyshire, he just wants to punish me. He—" she stopped abruptly. This outburst would go no way to convincing the attendant she was of sound mind. She drew in her breath.

"Please," she said calmly. "This is all a mistake. Just let me speak to someone."

The attendant gave her the tiniest hint of a smile. "You'll be taken to see the head physician in the morning. It's late. Now take off your dress and give it to me." She sat the colourless pile of clothing on the bed. "You'll find a clean nightshift in there."

Beth hesitated. Finally, seeing little alternative, she stepped out of the dress and handed it to the attendant.

All a mistake, she told herself as she stood shivering in her underskirts. In the morning, she would explain herself to the head physician. In the morning, she would be freed.

THE MORNING FELT as though it took an eternity to arrive. Beth lay on her back, staring at the cracked ceiling, the thin grey blanket pulled to her chin.

Throughout the night, footsteps echoed up and down the corridor in response to the shrieks and moans coming from the rooms surrounding her. Beth shivered, sleepless, hatred at her grandfather roiling under her skin.

She opened her eyes to see pale light filtering in through the small, rectangular window close to the ceiling. She was surprised to find she had slept, having spent most of the night staring in terror at the ceiling.

She sat up in bed, catching sight of the straps fastened to the sides of the bed. Restraints, Beth realised sickly. She was glad she had missed them in the dark of the previous night. They would have done little to help her sleepless state.

She tensed as the door to her tiny room clicked open. The sallow-faced attendant who had locked Beth in the previous night stood in the doorway. Her grey hair was pulled back sharply from her face and tucked neatly beneath a blue cap.

"Get dressed, Miss Thursday," she said. "You're to see Doctor Miller, after breakfast this morning."

Beth hurriedly threw back the covers, snatching

the grey dress from where she had hung it over the back of the bed.

"Yes," she said, doing her best to sound as calm as possible. "Of course." She buttoned up her dress and pulled on her stockings. "I don't need to eat. Perhaps I might see him now?"

The attendant chuckled humourlessly. "My, you are in a hurry. You'll see him when he's ready to see you." She nodded at Beth to follow her. "This way now. It's time for breakfast."

Beth followed her down the corridor to a hall lined with long wooden tables. The benches were filled with women all dressed in matching grey smocks, watched over by expressionless attendants. Beth closed her eyes, imagining herself back at the workhouse.

At the attendant's bidding, she slipped onto the end of one of the benches, keeping her eyes down. Across from her, an old woman was murmuring to herself, a girl to her right was crying silently. Beth glanced at her curiously, guessing her to be no older than thirteen or fourteen. Their eyes met for a moment and Beth hurriedly looked away. She could see the vicious red welts around the girl's wrists.

A bowl of watery porridge was placed in front of

her. Though her stomach was rolling, Beth forced down a few mouthfuls to steady herself.

Then she followed the attendant down the corridor towards Doctor Miller's office.

She practised drawing in long, steady breaths, forcing herself to focus.

The attendant rapped sharply on the door. "Sir? Elizabeth Thursday."

"Thank you. Bring her in." The doctor's voice was deep and gravelly.

Beth lifted her chin and pressed her shoulders back as she stepped into the office.

Doctor Miller was a large, red-faced man with round shoulders and an even rounder belly. His broadcloth waistcoat strained across his middle, the buttons threatening to fly free. He peered at Beth with small, dark eyes and gestured to the chair in front of his desk. He must have been seventy years old if he was a day.

"Miss Thursday. Sit, please."

Beth sat. She hesitated. Ought she to speak first? Tell the doctor everything he needed to know?

"How are you feeling today," he asked slowly, in a clear, patronising tone. Beth bristled, folding her hands in her lap and squeezing her fingers together.

"I feel just fine," Beth told him, in her calmest,

clearest voice. "Although I am rather put out at the injustice of all this."

Miller smiled beneath his grey moustache. "And what injustice would that be?"

Beth gritted her teeth. "The Earl of Derbyshire has no right to put me in here."

Miller nodded slowly. "His Lordship tells us you have been causing rather a great deal of trouble. He says you have been causing all manner of disturbances to him and his family. You ought to be grateful he is being generous enough to pay for your treatment. As you said, he has no obligation to do so."

Beth's fingers tightened around the arms of the chair.

"I just want to see my mother," she said with as much calmness as she could muster.

The physician gave her a thin smile. "Yes. You believe Lady Caroline is your mother, is that right?"

"I don't *believe* it," Beth said stiffly. "I know it."

The doctor gave a short chuckle that made the back of Beth's neck prickle with anger. "And how do you know this, Miss Thursday?" he asked.

Beth clenched her teeth. She knew that anything she said would be twisted into lies. Still, she felt a desperate need to tell her story.

"Lady Caroline visited me at the tailor's shop where I used to work," she said evenly. "She told me she was forced to give me up at birth."

She knew well, of course, that Lady Caroline had been forced to give her up between these very walls. Had Doctor Miller been the one to pull Beth from her mother's arms?

She felt a fresh rush of hatred for the man. She closed her eyes for a moment to steady herself.

Miller rubbed his shorn chin. "You were an orphan of Southwark Workhouse, is that correct?"

Beth bristled at the word *orphan*. For the first time in her life, she was certain she was not an orphan. She was not going to admit to being one just to appease the physician.

"I came from Southwark Workhouse, yes," she said stiffly. "Because that was where I was taken after I was pulled from my mother's arms as an infant." She looked squarely at Miller. If there was any hint of guilt within him, he hid it well.

"I imagine your life has been a difficult one," replied the Doctor. "A childhood in the workhouse. You must have dreamed for someone to come and save you. A wealthy mother, perhaps. A member of the nobility?"

Beth stared him down. "Lady Caroline came to me," she said sharply. "I did not go searching for her."

Miller nodded, his jowls moving up and down. "As you know, Lady Caroline also has a history of madness. Her father, the Earl, confirms she has never been married, nor given birth to any children."

"He's lying," Beth hissed.

"And why would he do that?"

"Because he doesn't want the shame of it to taint his name!" she spat. "He doesn't want to admit to the way he treated his own daughter!" She leaned forward in her chair. "He tried to buy my silence. Pay me to never speak of my relationship with him."

Miller nodded slowly. "We are well aware of your visits to the Earl's home. You hunted him down, did you not? An obsession."

"I did not *hunt him down*," Beth repeated icily. "Lady Caroline told me where she lived. I was simply going to visit my mother."

The doctor leant forward. "The Earl tells us that when you came to his house, you were in quite some state of distress. He says you evidently required food and shelter. And he was very generous in giving you a sum of money for food. And you repaid him by continuing to hound him and causing a scene at a private London club. It brought him no joy to have to bring you here," he said. "But perhaps you might begin to see that he had little choice. Lies cannot be allowed to breed. Can they?"

"It's him that's the liar!" she cried, the anger within her taking hold. She leapt to her feet. "He knows I'm not mad! He just wants me out of the way so he can pretend I don't exist!"

"Sit down, Miss Thursday. Or there will be consequences."

Gritting her teeth, Beth perched on the edge of the chair. She pinned her eyes on Mr Miller. "Tell the Earl I will never come near him again," she hissed. "I just want to know my mother is safe. I just want to know where she is."

THE ATTENDANT LED Beth back down the passage, her footsteps echoing in the cavernous passage. With each step, Beth felt her anger towards the Earl morphing into fear. Out of desperation, she had convinced herself that once she sat down with the physician, everything would be all right. She would explain herself, and the Earl of Derbyshire would be revealed as the villain he was.

But now she was filled with dread and hopelessness. She knew well that money talked.

And the Earl had money. Money he was willing to hand over to the Bedlam. No doubt Miller was in his pay as well. Money was all that mattered.

The attendant led Beth into a white-tiled room. Three iron bathtubs were lined up in a row, each of them empty. On the edges of the bath hung straps similar to those she had found on the side of her bed. Beth shivered at the sight of them.

The attendant did not take her to the tubs. Instead, she led her to a chair in the corner of the room.

Beth perched on the chair, knotting her fingers together. Her heart was racing. The attendant slid the pins from Beth's hair, letting her curls cascade down her back. She produced a pair of scissors from within her apron.

"What are you doing?" Beth stammered.

The attendant didn't reply. She sliced through a chunk of Beth's hair. It fluttered down to land at her feet.

"No," Beth spluttered. "Please. I don't want you to cut my hair. I..." she faded out. This was a foolish battle to fight, she knew. It was just hair, after all. It would grow back. She had best save her energy. Nonetheless, she felt tears welling behind her eyes as her curls gathered at her feet.

She swiped away a tear in embarrassment. "Why are you doing this?" she asked the attendant. The scissors squeaked around her ears.

"This will cool your mind," the attendant told her. "Doctor Miller hopes it will help you think more clearly."

Beth squeezed her eyes closed. Miller knew there was nothing wrong with her. This was all a sham. Just a way of taking the Earl's money.

She tightened her fingers around the arms of the chair. She felt utterly powerless.

A cold wind swept suddenly through the room, tickling the bare skin on the back of her neck. At the feel of it, the tears she had been holding back spilt suddenly down her cheeks.

Hacking off the last of Beth's long tresses, the attendant slid the scissors back into her apron. Her footsteps echoed as she made her way across the room, opening the door and murmuring to someone in the doorway.

She returned with a small vial of liquid.

"Drink this." She held it out to Beth.

Beth stiffened. She shook her head.

The woman sighed. "This is not optional, Miss Thursday. It's important you do as you're told. Everyone here has your best interests at heart." She nodded at the vial. "Now, are you going to cooperate? Or am I going to have to force you?"

Her body trembling, Beth took the vial from the woman's hand. The yellow liquid was murky and sour smelling. Her stomach rolled at the sensation. Closing her eyes, she tossed it down her throat, coughing violently at its bitter taste.

"There." The attendant gave her an unfriendly smile. "That wasn't so bad now, was it."

Beth felt herself gasping for breath. Her throat and stomach felt tight.

The attendant took her arm and led her back to her room. She pulled the chamber pot out from beneath the bed.

"Here," she said, "you'll be needing this."

As she spoke, Beth lurched forward, emptying her stomach violently into the pot. "What was that?" she coughed. "What did you give me."

The attendant watched with folded arms as Beth continued to cough, hunching over the bowl.

"Just a little castor oil," she said.

"Castor oil?"

The attendant leaned against the doorframe. When Beth finally stumbled back towards her bed, she reached down and took the chamber pot.

"It's like Doctor Miller always says, we need to

purge the illness from your body. Then your mind will be free."

Beth curled into a ball on her bed, burying her eyes against her knees. As she listened to the door close heavily behind the attendant, she realised her fear had grown into an all-encompassing terror. She had no way of fighting back against the powers that worked against her. And no one in this place cared that she had been wrongly incarcerated.

Then there was her fear for Lady Caroline. If the Earl was capable of throwing his granddaughter in here like this, what had he done to his daughter?

Beth stared through the narrow slit of the window, running her fingers through her hacked-at curls. She looked up, focusing on the fragile spear of light that was struggling through the window.

Somehow, she had to escape from this place. It was the only hope she had.

CHAPTER 20

For two weeks, Beth played the obedient patient, following the attendants soundlessly as they led her to and from the dining hall, to her meetings with Doctor Miller, for strolls around the gardens. And as she trailed them silently, her eyes were alert, seeking possible escape routes, trying to memorise the layout of the enormous hospital, commit the attendants' schedules to heart.

She even did her best to stay focused during her treatments; swallowing the castor oil without a word, and even managing to stay calm when they covered her skin in leeches for a round of bloodletting as though it were still the Tudor era.

One morning a fortnight after she first arrived at

the asylum, Beth sat in the sewing room, her needle darting furiously over the shift she was hemming. Her daily visits to the sewing room were her only saving grace; times when she could lose herself in a task she loved. When she was sewing, Beth was able to convince herself in a faint flicker of hope. Perhaps one day soon she might be free of this place and return to the life she had had before. She smiled wryly to herself at the thought. What she wouldn't give to spend her days doing slop work on the floor of her tenement.

But this morning her mind was filled with nothing but the immediate future. She knew well that after their time in the sewing room was up, she and the other women in her ward would be taken out to the garden. There they would be permitted to stroll the grounds to take in a little air.

And it was then that she would make her escape.

On her previous visits to the garden, Beth had been edging further and further away from the courtyard in which the patients wandered. Beyond the courtyard, she learned, was the rose garden; beyond that, the row of oak trees, and beyond that, the fence.

The fence was high, to be certain, but Beth was convinced it was scalable. Never mind that she had never climbed more than a staircase in her life. She felt certain that her determination and energy would be enough to propel her over the fence and into the freedom beyond.

Her heart was speeding with anticipation as they began to pack up the needles and threads. Around her, the other patients were noisy, some chatting to each other, others murmuring incoherently. One woman was belting out a hymn. Each of them was dressed in a shapeless grey dress, each of them had shorn hair that stuck out around their ears. How many of these women, Beth found herself wondering on a regular basis, had been wrongly incarcerated? How many of them were here because they had dared cross a powerful man like the Earl of Derbyshire?

She glanced out the window. The autumn day was grey, but as far as Beth could tell, the clouds had not yet opened. As she folded up the newly hemmed shift, she sent up a silent prayer that the rain would hold off. She knew they would not be permitted outside if the weather was bad.

To her relief, the attendants began to herd them towards the door.

"Come on then," one said gruffly. "Out you all go before it starts to rain."

Beth kept her eyes down, doing her best to blend into the sea of grey around her.

The two attendants led the women out to the courtyard. Orange leaves had begun to blanket the paving. Beth kept walking, out onto the damp grass.

"You stay where we can see you, Miss Thursday," the attendant called after her.

Beth nodded obediently. She knew the attendants had come to expect her to roam about. They would surely think nothing of it. She had been nothing but obedient so far. She hoped she had lulled them into a false sense of security.

With the others still in her line of sight, Beth approached the rose garden. Once she reached the edge of the plot, she could dart off into the oak trees. They would likely give her enough cover to sprint towards the fence.

She felt anxious and jittery. She forced herself not to look back at the other patients, knowing such an act would draw attention to her.

Here was the edge of the rose garden. There was the line of oak trees.

Beth sucked in her breath and ran. Her skirts held up above her knees, she began to sprint towards the back of the garden. She could see the fence between the thick trunks of the oak trees.

"You there!"

The man's voice startled her, but Beth kept running. She grabbed the bars of the fence and tried to scramble up.

Footsteps pelted towards her. And Beth felt firm hands around her, yanking her off the fence. "Let go of me!" she cried. She kicked wildly, trying to see who had a hold of her. "You can't keep me in here like this!"

The man set her down, not releasing his grip on her arm. Beth whirled around, catching sight of the groundskeeper.

"Please," she tried again. "Let me go. I don't belong in here. A man is trying to punish me. The Earl of Derbyshire..." she faded out, realizing how mad she sounded.

The groundskeeper marched her back inside without saying a word.

BY THE TIME they reached the main building, two of the attendants had caught up with them. They each took a hold of one of Beth's arms. Doctor Miller strode down the corridor towards them. "What happened?"

"She tried to escape, sir," said one of the attendants. "The groundskeeper caught her at the back fence."

Miller rubbed his chin, eyeing Beth as though she was an animal who had tried to break free from its cage.

"Restrain her in her room," he told them, his voice empty of emotion.

"No!" Beth cried, panic shooting through her. "No, please!"

The attendants led her into her room and forced her onto the bed. Beth thrashed wildly as they grabbed one wrist each, forcing her into the restraints that were attached to the edge of the bed.

"Calm yourself," hissed one of the attendants. "Or you're just going to make things worse."

The buckles clattered loudly as the straps closed tight around Beth's skin. She kicked harder as they moved to her ankles, pinning her in place and securing the straps tightly. A sob escaped her as she felt herself unable to move.

The attendants left without another word.

PINNED TO HER BED, her body trembling in fear, Beth spent the whole night staring at the ceiling. She sent up prayer after prayer for just a few moments of sleep; anything to ease the pain in her arms and legs, and the even greater pain in her heart.

But sleep refused to come, and when the first light flickered through the window, there were more footsteps coming towards her room.

Beth closed her eyes, feeling fresh tears prick her eyes. She lay motionless, the skin around her wrists and ankles stinging in the places it had rubbed against the restraints.

The door swung open and in strode the two attendants who had strapped her to her bed the day before. Without speaking, they unfastened the buckles and pulled Beth to her feet. Her aching legs gave way beneath her and the two women yanked her back to her feet.

"Where are you taking me?" she coughed, her throat rough with tears.

"Doctor Miller is most unhappy with your progress," said one of the attendants as they walked. She kept her eyes directly ahead, not looking at Beth. "And he's extremely disappointed at your behaviour yesterday. He feels a new treatment would be appropriate."

They led Beth into the white-tiled room in which she'd had her hair cut. This time, one of the narrow bathtubs was filled with water. Mr Miller stood beside the tub, a thin smile on his face.

"You'll feel much better after this, Miss Thursday," he said smoothly. "Much more clear-headed, I assure you. I feel rather sure you'll be making no more ill-advised escape attempts."

One of the attendants unbuttoned Beth's dress and pulled it over her head, leading her towards the bath in her shift.

Beth stiffened. Before she could protest, the attendants lifted her off her feet and lowered her into the tub.

Beth let out a cry of shock, the icy water stealing her breath. She tried to scramble out, but the attendants kept their hands firmly pressed down on her shoulders. They reached for the straps and fastened them around her wrists, pinning her in place.

Beth felt the cold closing in around her. Felt it stealing the energy from her muscles, felt it stealing her urge to fight.

She heard another set of footsteps clicking their way across the tiles.

"Ah, glad you're just in time, Doctor Field," she heard Miller say distantly. "This is quite a troublesome patient. Best you keep an eye on her. She doesn't respond well."

CHAPTER 21

Beth was dimly aware of being carried back to her room. She felt herself being placed on the bed. Felt the thin blanket lifted up to her chin. She blinked. She could see two attendants in their white dresses and the long black coat of the physician. She stiffened, shuffling back in her bed to get as far away from him as possible. A violent shiver racked her body.

"Fetch her more blankets at once," the physician told the attendants. His voice was soft and gentle. "And I want one of you to stay with her. See she suffers no lasting effects."

Not Miller, Beth realised. She tried to sit but felt drained and heavy. She let her head sink back against the pillow.

"Steady," the physician said, crouching to look in her eyes. "Just relax now."

Beth blinked again, trying to focus on his face. It was smooth and unlined with youth, his coffee-coloured hair appeared slightly overgrown at his ears. He hovered over Beth's bed, peering down at her with concern in his eyes.

"Who are you?" she managed. Her voice came out husky, her throat on fire.

"My name is Nathan Field," he said, his voice low. "I'm the new junior physician here at Bethlem."

"Why are you in my room?" Beth rubbed her eyes, not entirely sure she wasn't dreaming.

"I take the wellbeing of the patients here very seriously," he told her. "And I'm concerned about you."

"It was you who came into the bathroom," Beth said. "It was you Doctor Miller was speaking to."

"Yes."

"Why have I not seen you before?" Beth pulled her blanket tighter around her as her shivering intensified.

The door clicked open and the attendant reappeared with an armful of blankets. She began to pile them over Beth's body. She felt a little of the chill begin to disappear.

"I've been working in the men's wards for the past two years," Mr Field told her. "But I've since been transferred." His grey eyes met hers. "How do you feel?"

Beth let out her breath. "How do you imagine I feel?"

"Not good, I assume."

Was that regret in his voice? She couldn't tell.

"You need to rest," he told her. "I will have one of the attendants stay with you a while. Make sure you have everything you need."

IN THE MORNING, Beth awoke alone in her room. Her throat was burning, but the violent shivering of the night before had eased. Her limbs felt heavy but far more energised than they had the previous day.

Nathan Field, she presumed, had been nothing but a water-induced dream. She knew it was too much to expect any form of kindness or understanding in this place.

Today she was to visit Doctor Miller again. She was to sit opposite him in that chair beside his desk and listen to him spout lie after lie, each one paid for by the Earl of Derbyshire.

Miller had been right, she thought wryly. The ice baths had helped clear her head. Because right now she could see with clarity that the only way forward was to obey. Do anything else and it would cost her life. Though the attendants did their best to keep them away, everyone here knew of the cemetery behind the groundskeepers' shed where they buried those who had not been strong enough to survive.

What would happen if she was to agree with the physicians, she found herself wondering? What if she just nodded along and told Miller that yes, the Earl of Derbyshire was right, she was just a poor workhouse orphan in search of a mother? Would she be released?

It was a gamble, Beth knew. But perhaps it was a gamble she ought to take.

To do such a thing felt like a betrayal to Lady Caroline. But Lady Caroline, wherever she was, was in trouble, Beth was sure of it. And she would be in a far better position to help her from outside these walls.

Besides, Beth was not sure she had it in her to go through the ice bath again. For a few fragile, fleeting moments, she had felt herself close to death.

She walked towards Doctor Miller's office on unsteady legs. The attendant kept a firm hand around her arm, preventing her from falling, or preventing her from running, Beth was unsure.

She thought to tell the woman there was no need to restrain her. She had made up her mind. She was going to agree with everything Miller said.

Yes, she was a poor workhouse orphan, driven mad by the need to know her mother.

Yes, she had convinced herself she was Lady Caroline's daughter in an act of desperation.

Yes, she had caused no end of trouble to the poor Earl of Derbyshire and his family.

But when Beth stepped through the door, her lips parted with shock. Beside Miller sat the young doctor who had been so kind to her last night.

She blinked. Doctor Field had not been a figment of her imagination. He was real and solid and staring intently at Beth with warm grey eyes.

"How do you feel today, Miss Thursday?" asked Miller.

Beth hesitated. "I'm well sir," she said shortly.

Miller nodded towards the young man. "This is your new physician, Doctor Nathan Field."

As Beth opened her mouth to tell Miller they had already met, Field's eyes caught hers. She stopped abruptly. And in that wordless glance, she realised that Field had accompanied Beth back from the ice tubs without the senior physician's permission. He had risked his position and reputation to make sure she was safe.

She gave him a short nod of greeting. "How do you do, Doctor?"

Her heart had quickened, Beth realised. The presence of Field had made her suddenly uncertain of her plan to declare herself mad. Why? She couldn't place it. Was it that she did not want Field to think her unwell? Or perhaps, in some strange way, his presence helped reassure her of the injustice of the situation.

She wasn't sure. She only knew there was no way she was going to make things easier for Miller and the Earl.

Miller leant back in his chair, folding his hands across his wide stomach. "Perhaps we might start at the beginning today, Miss Thursday. Tell us about your time at Southwark Workhouse."

Beth bristled. She knew what he wanted to hear, of course. A tragic tale of orphans pining over their long-lost mothers. She would tell him none of it.

"Do you remember much of your time at the workhouse?" he asked.

"Of course," she said, speaking strong and clear, despite the burning in her throat. "I spent every day of my life in the place until I was eight years old."

"What kind of memories do you have of the place, Miss Thursday?" asked Doctor Field.

Beth hesitated, considering her answer. There was something about Nathan Field that made her want to speak more openly. Made her want to tell him everything about her memories of the workhouse. Made her want to say *I spent every day of those eight years longing for my mother.*

But she could do none of that in Miller's presence, of course. Do so and she would give him everything he wanted to hear.

FREED from the confines of Miller's office, Beth escaped to the sewing room. She sat in the corner with a needle and thread in her hand, letting her mind still as she embroidered an intricate floral design on the hem of a handkerchief.

She looked up at the sound of footsteps coming towards her. She was surprised to see Nathan Field approaching. Not once had she ever seen Doctor Miller set foot into the sewing room. Or anywhere the patients congregated, for that matter. No, the

Bedlam head physician liked to oversee proceedings from the safety of his office.

Doctor Field smiled at her. "Miss Thursday. How are you feeling?"

Beth managed a small smile. "A little better. Thank you Doctor."

He looked down at the neat embroidery. "That's fine work. You must be quite a seamstress."

"I was a tailor's apprentice," Beth told him, making the final stitch on the design. "Before…" she faded out, folding the handkerchief and tucking it in her pocket.

"I see. You must be very eager to return to that life."

Beth laughed humourlessly. "That life is long gone. I'm sure you know that as well as I do."

Field titled his head in thought, a swathe of dark hair falling over one eye. He nodded towards the garden. "It's a fine day. Would you care for a walk in the garden? I think it would do you good." He gave her a small smile. "And I'm not sure how many more sunny days we can count on this year."

Beth nodded. Despite her sharpness, she felt oddly safe around Doctor Field. And that was a feeling she had not experienced once in the two months since the Earl had seen her committed.

She nodded. "Yes. Thank you. I would like that very much."

The sun was shining despite the cold, with a bright blue sky stretching overhead. Beth squinted as she made her way out into the garden with Nathan Field. She lifted her face to the sky, feeling the soft warmth of the sun against her cheeks. It felt as though it was bringing back a little of the life that had drained from her after her time in the ice bath.

Doctor Field walked with his arms folded behind his back, a faint frown creasing the bridge of his nose. The trees on either side of the path were bright with autumn colours.

"Tell me what brought you here," he sanctioned after several moments of silence.

Beth raised her eyebrows. "You're my physician," she said, sharper than she had intended. "Surely you know why I'm here. Surely Doctor Miller has told you."

Field didn't speak at once and Beth regretted her terseness.

"I would like to hear it from you," he said after a moment. "Outside of the good Doctor Miller's presence."

Beth smiled crookedly. "And would you like to hear the truth, Doctor Field? Or would you prefer the version your superior has convinced himself of?"

This brought a long silence from Field. His polished black shoes clicked rhythmically along the path. His frown deepened slightly.

Beth eyed him curiously. She wondered what he was thinking.

"I want the truth," he said finally, his eyes meeting hers. "I always want the truth."

Beth smiled wryly to herself. She had told the truth before in this place, and what good had it done her? But there was something about this man. Perhaps it was her desperate need to be able to trust someone here. Perhaps it was her desperate need to be seen for who she really was. Or perhaps it was how he looked at her so intently. It felt as though he was looking into her very soul.

"The truth," she began, "is that Lord Derbyshire threw me in here for causing trouble. I'm not mad." She let out a cold laugh. "I'm sure all your patients tell you that."

Field gave her a small smile. He nodded for her to continue.

"I grew up in the workhouse," she said. "I never knew my mother or father. I believed I was an orphan. But then one day, Lord Derbyshire's daughter came to me and told me I was her child. She said she had been forced to give me up – right here in Bethlem Asylum.

"When the Earl's men found out Lady Caroline had made contact with me, they had her taken away. I was trying to find her when his Lordship threw me in here. Told them I was mad. It was his way of getting rid of me, you see. His way of ensuring I brought no further shame to his family."

Field did not speak for a long time. "I see," he said finally.

Beth waited. Surely he had more to say on the matter than *I see?*

Did he believe her words? It was impossible to tell.

Finally, Doctor Field looked up. He looked at her squarely, his grey eyes full of compassion. The sight of them brought a lump to Beth's throat. When was the last time someone had treated her with kindness? When was the last time someone had looked at her as more than a madwoman who ought to be hidden from society?

"I'm sorry, Miss Thursday," he said. "For all you've endured in this place. I know many of the treatments here are… unpleasant, to say the least."

Beth raised her eyebrows. "I'm surprised to hear you say such a thing, Doctor. If you feel that way, why take a position in this place?"

Field gave her a small smile that made something warm in her chest. "I firmly believe those who are not of sound mind should be given appropriate care, Miss Thursday. And I can do far more for those people in this institution than I can anywhere else."

NATHAN FIELD's mind was racing as he let himself into his Clerkenwell townhouse. He shrugged off his greatcoat and hung it on the hook beside the front door, along with his top hat.

He knew he had spoken too openly with Beth Thursday that afternoon. Knew he ought never to have told her the way he felt about the treatments. But the words had come spilling out without him having any thought of it.

Nathan knew the cardinal rule of working in such an institution, of course – not to get personally involved with one's patients. In his two years of practising, he had managed to do so successfully. But Beth Thursday was different. He couldn't help but feel drawn to her. However dangerous it may be.

He followed the aroma of meat and spices, into his kitchen. His daily, Annie, was hunched over a stew pot with a wooden spoon in her hand.

She looked up at the sound of his footsteps. "Good evening, Doctor Field. Your supper's almost ready for you."

Nathan smiled, his stomach groaning. "Thank you, Annie." He glanced at his watch. "You're late leaving. Please, go home. I can manage perfectly fine on my own from here."

"Thank you, sir. There's wine on the table if you wish. And a little bread and butter."

Nathan bid his maid good evening, then carried his bowl of stew to the sitting room. He tossed another log on the fire and sank into his favourite armchair, the bowl resting against his chest and a large glass of wine on the side table.

He took a mouthful of stew and stared into the flames. Watching the fire always relaxed him.

There were many evenings when he came home from Bethlem and felt the need to stare into the fire. Anything to clear his mind of the horrors he had witnessed at the asylum. Even after two years, he struggled to distance himself from the wails of the patients as they were thrashed and restrained against their desperate pleas to be released from horrors that were inflected.

He knew the arguments in favour of such a practice, of course. Older physicians like his superior believed staunchly in such techniques, believing them the only way to calm the mind, to expel madness from the body. But these were arguments that did not resonate with him. Medicine and mental care was changing.

Watching Beth Thursday being subjected to the ice baths had almost been more than Nathan could bear. He couldn't place why. What was it about Miss Thursday that was drawing him to her?

Nathan knew he would be punished severely if Doctor Miller discovered that he had followed Beth and the attendants back to her room. Such behaviour was wildly inappropriate, of course. A male doctor and female inmate. But he had felt a desperate need to ensure she would recover.

And would you like to hear the truth, Doctor Field? Or would you prefer the version your superior has convinced himself of?

Her words continued to circle through his mind.

While she was certainly not the first patient to have claimed she had been wrongly incarcerated,

Nathan had seen few who had done so as calmly and coherently as Beth Thursday.

He brought his glass to his lips, feeling the warmth as the alcohol slid down his throat. He untied his cravat and tossed it on the side table.

He had taken the position at Bethlem because he wanted to make a difference. Wanted to improve people's lives. He knew of the kind of treatments that went on in such an institution, long before he had started his university studies.

His own mother had been held in such an establishment, subjected to water treatments, purging and regular beatings. As a child, Nathan had not known the details of these treatments but had been very aware of the fading light in his mother's eyes.

After her death, he had dedicated himself to learning all he could about illnesses of the mind. And the more he learned, the more certain he became that such brutal treatments were of little value.

Nonetheless, he knew he had been wrong to share such sentiments with a patient. Nathan knew he was letting his attraction to Miss Thursday cloud his judgement. After all, that was what it was, wasn't it? Attraction? Nathan knew there was little point denying it, especially to himself.

CHAPTER 22

Beth awoke the next morning feeling something close to optimism. Perhaps it was the sunshine that had soaked into her pale skin the day before. Or perhaps it was the company.

The truth, Doctor Field had said. *I always want the truth.*

And was it possible that he had believed her story?

She kept watch throughout the day for the young physician, looking for him as she ate her meals, as she sewed her petticoats, as she walked with the other patients in the garden.

Somewhere in the back of her mind was a flicker of hope that he would come to her and tell her he believed her. Tell her she was free.

But there was no sign of him.

When she was returned to her room in the evening without so much as a glimpse of him, the old sinking in her chest returned with force.

NATHAN SAT IN HIS OFFICE, listening to Doctor Miller's footsteps disappear down the corridor towards the physician's chambers at the far end of the asylum.

The sun had long dipped beneath the horizon. Nathan had been sitting at his desk for what felt like hours, not bothering to turn on the lamps, watching as the shadows stretched and bathed the room.

His mind was racing, his thoughts fixated on the patient he had visited with Doctor Miller that afternoon.

A slender, dark-haired woman in her thirties, whose chopped curls tickled the back of her neck, much the same way Beth Thursday's did.

The woman had been at the asylum for almost three months, Miller had told him, incarcerated for the second time after a long history of madness. Nowadays, she was refusing to leave her bed, and barely ate the meals that were brought to her.

Nathan had felt his heart quicken as he had read through the woman's records.

"The daughter of the Earl of Derbyshire?" he had repeated. "This is the woman Elizabeth Thursday claims to be her mother."

Miller shot him a wordless glare. A glare that told him not to ask questions.

"Miss Thursday doesn't know Lady Caroline is here, does she?" Nathan questioned, anger making his voice rise.

"Of course not," said Miller. "That would cause no end of trouble. It would be no good for either of them."

Nathan said nothing. But as he looked at Lady Caroline, he recognised the narrow face, the dark, haunted eyes.

And he knew, with certainty, that Beth Thursday was telling the truth.

He sat now in his office, spinning a pen between his fingers.

Miller was not blind. Surely he could see the resemblance between the two women. Surely he knew Miss Thursday's story was the truth.

There could be no doubt about it. Miller was taking the Earl of Derbyshire's money in exchange for incarcerating his troublesome daughter and granddaughter. The thought left a sick feeling in the pit of Nathan's stomach.

He couldn't just accept this. Couldn't pretend to be ignorant. Who else had Miller seen fit to incarcerate for the sake of a few pounds?

Had Miller played a part in ensuring Lady Caroline no longer ventured from her room? Had he beaten the woman down in order to keep mother and daughter from laying eyes on each other?

Nathan's fist tightened around the pen. What was he to do about this? As the junior physician, he had little power, regardless of whether he was in the right or not.

Full of nervous energy, he began to pace. This was about professional integrity, yes. But he knew there was more to it. He knew it was also about the way Beth Thursday made his heart quicken. The way he longed to hold her to him. The way he longed to make her his. These were feelings he had done his best to deny. But he could do that no longer.

Making his decision, Nathan snatched the unlit lamp from his desk and headed out of his office.

Beth sat up in bed at the sound of footsteps approaching. Her heart began to thunder. Surely they wouldn't subject her to the ice baths again. Not now in the middle of the night.

The door opened a crack to reveal the tall silhouette of Nathan Field.

Beth felt her muscles relax. She climbed hurriedly out of bed and threw on her dress.

"Forgive me," he said. "I know I shouldn't be coming to you in the night like this. But I need to speak with you, without Doctor Miller around."

Beth squinted in the pale light of the lamp in his hand. "You need to speak to me?"

"Yes. May I come in? It's best we speak in private."

Beth nodded. Doctor Field closed the door behind him

"I'm sorry I was unable to call on you today," he said. "I had many other patients to attend to."

Beth nodded. "It's all right."

"I know you're telling the truth about your mother," Field said suddenly.

Beth exhaled sharply, feeling her heart jump. "What? You do? How?"

He gave her a small smile. "I've enough experience to know when a patient is truly unwell."

Beth rubbed her eyes, overwhelmed with relief. "I'm glad you can see that," she said, her voice cracking. Would the word of young Doctor Field be enough to get her out of this place? She knew it was unlikely. But there was something endlessly calming about being believed. For the first time in months, she did not feel utterly alone.

"I'm so sorry for all you've endured in this institution," Field said, his voice thickening with emotion. "I wish I could have put a stop to it."

Beth managed a small smile. She did not want this kind man to feel guilty on account of her.

"It wasn't your doing," she said softly. "I know that."

Field lowered his eyes. Beth could tell her words had done little to convince him.

"There's something else you should know," he said after a moment. "Your mother, Lady Caroline… She's here at Bethlem."

CHAPTER 23

Caroline curled up in the corner of her bed, her knees drawn to her chest. Her arms and legs were aching after the thrashing she had received that morning. It felt as though every inch of her skin was covered with purple and red bruises.

Once a week, Miller would press her to admit to her mistakes.

Yes, she could say, *I sought out a stranger at a tailor's shop and convinced myself she was my long-lost daughter.*

Denying Beth's existence, she knew, would give her a chance to get out of this place. But she would never do such a thing. Certainly not now, after she had spent so much time with her daughter. She would die confined before she told them what they wanted to hear.

Though it had been seventeen years since she was last incarcerated at Bethlem, the memories still hung thick in the air. The beatings and the ice baths, Caroline could handle. But the constant reliving of the past was true torture.

The months before her child had been born, had been terrifying, both expecting and fearing the worst. And the worst had come, when the attendants had lifted the child from her arms and told her it was for the best. Caroline's screams had woken her sleeping baby and the shrieks of both of them had echoed down the passages.

The Earl had allowed Caroline to return home, on condition she never spoke of the child again. And not once in those seventeen years did Caroline ever speak of her daughter. But there was not a day that Beth was not in her thoughts.

She supposed her regular excursions without her lady's maid had drawn her father's attention. No doubt the Earl had instructed his footmen to follow her, and they had drawn their own conclusions.

Caroline had seen herself in the contours of Beth's face from the moment she had laid eyes on her. While it filled her with joy that she and her daughter might share such a strong resemblance, she knew it had also likely been the cause of their undoing.

And yet Caroline couldn't bring herself to regret her actions. Perhaps she would be imprisoned here for the rest of her life, but at least she'd had the opportunity to spend those few precious days with her daughter. At least Beth knew she had not been abandoned. At least she knew how much her mother cared for her. At least she knew the truth.

Caroline opened her eyes at a soft knocking on the door. Had she imagined it? No one knocked on the doors in here. Miller and the attendants just barrelled their way inside whenever they saw fit. The knock came again.

"Lady Caroline? Are you awake?" The voice was gentle. A man's voice.

Curiously, Caroline climbed from the bed, tugging her thin grey shawl around her shoulders.

"Who's there?" she called.

The door unlocked from the outside and creaked open to reveal the young physician, Doctor Field.

At his side stood Beth, wearing the grey skirt of the asylum patients. Caroline stared, unable to make sense of all she was seeing. This couldn't be real, surely. It had to be an illusion. Perhaps she had finally succumbed to the madness Miller insisted was lying within her.

Beth rushed forward and threw her arms around her tightly. Caroline's breath left her. Her daughter's embrace was tight and fierce. And very real.

"Why are you here, Beth?" Caroline asked, the joy of seeing her daughter again tempered by the horror of the situation. "What happened? Have they locked you up?"

Beth clutched Caroline's hands. "Your father. I confronted him. At a club in the city. I asked him what he had done to you. And he had his men lock me up. And then they brought me here. Told everyone I was mad. But Doctor Field, he believed me. He believes *us*."

Caroline frowned, her thoughts knocking together. Nothing of Beth's story made sense. "You saw my father?"

"Yes. I went to the address on your calling card. His Lordship tried to have his footman pay to keep away. I saw the portrait in the stairwell. And then your father's carriage nearly ran me down outside the club. When I saw him get out of the coach, I knew immediately who he was."

Caroline exhaled sharply. "Oh, Beth." She pulled her daughter close, ignoring the ache in her bruised

THE ASYLUM DAUGHTER

arms. "I'm so sorry. This is all my fault. You ought never to have been caught up in any of it. I ought never to have come looking for you in the first place."

Beth stepped back, gripping Caroline's hands firmly. "Of course you should!" she cried. "You're my mother! And I've spent my whole life wanting to know who you were. Who *I* am. And now I've finally found you, I would never change any of it."

At her daughter's kind words, Caroline's tears spilt. Since the day she had been dragged away from Beth at the hotel, she had wildly regretted hunting her daughter down. And she had had no idea just how terribly Beth had been caught up in this whole terrible mess. Had never imagined the Earl could be so horrible as to lock up his grandchild in the same manner as he had his daughter. And yet, after all of it, Beth was happy she had come looking. Caroline felt an overwhelming swell of love.

She pressed her palms to Beth's cheeks. "How are they treating you here, my darling?" She was afraid of the answer. But she needed to know.

Beth managed a small smile that didn't reach her eyes. And in that feeble attempt at a smile, Caroline could see that she had not been the only one subjected to the horrors within the walls of the asylum. Hatred welled inside her. Hatred of her father. Hatred of Doctor Miller.

But then Beth said, "Doctor Field has been very kind to me. He listened to me. Took the time to hear my story. And he knows you and I are telling the truth."

Caroline blinked away fresh tears. They had someone on their side, at least. She knew well that Nathan Field had little sway in this place. She had seen him argue with Miller on more than one occasion. And the senior physician always won out. Still, Caroline reasoned, Doctor Field had brought her and her daughter together. And for that, she would always be grateful.

BETH SAT on the edge of the bed beside her mother, their fingers intertwined. Tears gathered in her throat; an odd mixture of happiness and grief.

"I've not seen you in the sewing room," she said. "Or in the garden. Why not?"

Lady Caroline squeezed her hand. "I'd given up, Beth. I thought my father had won. I thought, after finally finding you, I had lost you again forever. I saw no reason to get out of bed." She wiped her tears away. "But you can be sure that tomorrow I will be there. I'm going to stay by your side as much as I can."

"Forgive me," said Doctor Field. "But you must be getting back to your room, Miss Thursday. The attendants will be doing their rounds shortly. And I'm sure I need not tell you there will be trouble for all of us if anyone finds out about this."

Beth nodded reluctantly. "Yes, of course." She pulled her mother into a tight embrace. "Things are going to be all right," she said, her voice wavering. "Somehow. We'll find a way to get out of here. Together."

She followed Doctor Field back down the passage, stopping outside the door to her room.

"How long have you known she was here?" she asked, her voice low.

"I only discovered it this evening," he whispered. "I came to see you as soon as I could."

Beth met his eyes. "You could lose your job."

Field tilted his hair, his dark hair falling over one eye. "Perhaps. But…" he sighed. "What Doctor Miller is doing is not right. What he's put you and your mother through, it's…" he faded out, looking at Beth with apologetic eyes.

She felt a sudden urge to throw her arms around

him and never let go. Instead, she straightened her shoulders and gave him a small smile. "Thank you," she said. "Thank you so much. You've no idea what it means to me to see my mother again. And to know someone believes my story."

Field shook his head. "It's not enough. You and your mother should not be in here, Miss Thursday. And I'm going to do everything I can to make sure you're released."

CHAPTER 24

Caroline opened her eyes and looked up at the shaft of sunlight filtering into her room. For the first time since her return to this awful house of horrors, she felt a burst of hope.

She had lost the last of her optimism at almost the very moment her father had walked her through these doors again. It had all felt achingly familiar; the lifeless white walls, the chilled tiles of the bathroom, the wails and cries coming from within the cells. At the sound of it, Caroline was a terrified sixteen-year-old again, desperate not to lose her child.

But she had lost her child for a second time, again at the hands of her father.

Caroline had given up. She knew, deep within herself, that her father would not be bringing her back home. She had made her decision to turn down her suitors, to live as a spinster, to spend her life searching for her lost child. And for that, she would pay. She was nothing to her father but a beast of shame. She knew for certain he would never return to the asylum to collect her.

But now, for the first time since she had arrived, Caroline climbed out of bed of her own volition. Her heart was beating with fresh enthusiasm. She was still a prisoner, yes, but she had found Beth again. Found her in the worst of ways, yes, but they had a physician who believed their story. And that had to be worth something.

Today, Caroline was to see Doctor Miller for their weekly meeting. She found herself oddly looking forward to it. Today would be different. Today she would let Miller see that he had not defeated her. She would make it clear to him that she would keep fighting, until both she and her daughter were free.

She took her seat in Miller's office and looked him squarely in the eye. If this man was also treating her daughter, if Beth had told the same story – which Caroline knew she had – it meant that Miller knew the two women were telling the truth. It meant he knew the Earl to be a liar. And it meant he was keeping her locked up in order to take a nobleman's money. Was he even putting the money into the asylum's funds, she found herself wondering? Or was he keeping the money for himself?

"Good morning, Lady Caroline," said Miller, easing himself into his chair. "I must say you look rather well today. Good to see the treatments are beginning to have an effect."

Caroline didn't answer. She looked him straight in the eye, unflinching.

The door creaked suddenly, and Doctor Field stepped inside. "Pardon me," he said, glancing between Caroline and Doctor Miller. He slipped wordlessly into the chair beside his senior. Caroline tried to catch his eye, but Doctor Field kept his eyes averted, deliberately avoiding her gaze. Nonetheless, she was glad he was here.

"I thought today we might speak about your relationship with your father," said Doctor Miller.

Caroline fixed hard eyes on him. "I don't think so. Perhaps today we might speak about my daughter. Elizabeth. Perhaps I might tell you about her." Caroline drew in her breath, forcing herself to remain calm. She knew that if she said too much, she would put Field's job in jeopardy. She could not do such a thing, after all he had done for her and Beth.

"Very well," said Doctor Miller. "Tell me about Elizabeth, Lady Caroline."

How easily he spoke her daughter's name, Caroline realised bitterly. How dismissive he was of the whole matter. And the whole time he had been keeping Beth prisoner just a few rooms away. Anger boiled inside her.

"I expect you know more about Elizabeth than you are letting on," she spat, her rage tearing itself free. "I know who you are. I know what you've done. You're nothing but a money-hungry monster—"

She stopped abruptly. Miller's face had started to flush crimson.

She had said too much, Caroline knew. Had let herself lose control. And yet she was surprised to have elicited such a reaction from the physician. Surely in his time at Bethlem he had been subjected to worse than that?

Mr Miller grappled at his cravat, gasping for air. He clawed desperately at his chest.

Caroline stood abruptly, watching in shock as her chair toppled to the floor behind her.

Doctor Field was on his feet, rushing to Miller's side. The older man slumped forward, his heavy figure thudding against the desk.

Field hurried for the door, ushering Caroline out

into the corridor. As she left the room, she looked back at Doctor Miller's still form. She stood with her back pressed to the wall, her heart beating fast. Had she just witnessed a man die?

Field raced down the corridor, calling for assistance.

Attendants hurried into the office, ignoring Caroline. She hovered uncertainly. Never before had she been left alone like this in the confines of the asylum. Ought she to use this opportunity to find Beth? Could they take this opportunity to escape?

As she was about to dart down the hall, she felt a hand around her wrist. "I'll see you back to your room, Lady Caroline," Doctor Field said gently, releasing his grip.

"Is he dead?" she managed, though she already knew the answer.

Field nodded. "Yes. I'm afraid so.

Caroline hesitated. She had hated Miller, yes, but she had not wished him dead. "What happened?" she dared to ask.

"His heart, I assume. His age. His condition. It is not unlikely."

Caroline swallowed heavily. She heard her own bitter words, spat out at the doctor.

You're nothing but a money-hungry monster...

The last words he was ever to hear.

"It was not your fault," Mr Field said calmly as though reading her mind.

Caroline managed a small smile. She was not entirely sure she believed him. She wrapped her arms around herself.

"Please, Doctor Field," she said. "Will you take me to see my daughter?"

CHAPTER 25

*B*eth sat in the chair opposite Field's desk. His office was much smaller than Doctor Miller's, and far messier. Beth couldn't help but smile at the empty teacups and pencils scattered across the table.

"I suspect you have heard the news of Doctor Miller's passing yesterday."

Beth nodded. "Yes. My mother told me. I'm sorry." She meant it, she realised. She had not liked Miller a scrap. But she still felt bad about his passing.

Field gave her a small nod. He folded his hands on the desk in front of him. "With Doctor Miller's passing, the asylum has seen fit to offer me his position as senior physician."

Beth felt a small smile on her lips. If anyone

deserved such a promotion, it was Field. How would things change with the kindly young physician in charge? He knew her to be of sound mind, so surely he would not subject her to further ice baths. Surely he would no longer have her beaten, restrained, or forced to swallow castor oil. Surely she might be permitted to see her mother.

It was a dismal state of affairs, the two of them imprisoned and institutionalised at the will of the Earl. But at least they were confined together.

"You're being released, Miss Thursday," said Doctor Field. "As is your mother."

Beth stared for a moment, hardly able to believe what she was hearing. "Released?" she repeated.

Nathan smiled, his grey eyes lighting up. "Yes. I know your grandfather has paid well for your… treatment. But I cannot in good faith continue to treat you – or accept his money – when both you and Lady Caroline are of sound mind."

"Thank you," she coughed. "Thank you so much." She felt at once both exhausted and exhilarated.

"There's no need to thank me, Miss Thursday. I'll have an attendant bring you the clothes you were wearing when you were brought here. You may leave whenever you wish to do so."

Beth swallowed the tears of happiness that were

threatening. She managed a small nod, rising from her chair as Doctor Field did the same. He pushed open the door, his eyes meeting hers. And unable to hold herself back, Beth threw her arms around him and squeezed tightly.

For a moment, he stood motionless, as though taken aback by her forwardness. Then his arms slid around her and he held her tightly, as though he never wanted to let her go.

CHAPTER 26

Beth stood outside the gates of the asylum, her arm looped through Lady Caroline's. She lifted her face to the pale sun and inhaled deeply. With each breath, she felt her life returning to her. She had freedom. And she had her mother. A broad smile stretched across her face and she stretched her arms up towards the sun.

"I have nowhere to go," she told Lady Caroline finally. "Mr Whitaker's shop, it was taken by his creditors." She almost laughed. She had not a place in the world to go, but somehow it didn't matter. All that mattered was that she and her mother were together. And that they were free.

Caroline squeezed her arm. "Truly, Beth," she said, "I have no place to go either. I can't go back to the family home. I've no idea what my father will do if he discovers you and I have been freed."

Beth nodded. She knew her mother was right. His Lordship was capable of anything. She had no desire to see him ever again.

Catching sight of Beth's concerned expression, Lady Caroline squeezed her arm and smiled. "He'll not find us. I'll make sure of that. Even if he bothered to visit the asylum to check on us, which I strongly doubt, you know Doctor Field will do all he can to keep us safe."

Beth smiled to herself, the thought of Nathan Field leaving a warmth inside her.

"We have money," Lady Caroline assured her. "I have bank accounts my family is not aware of. I make sure of it, just in case. Tonight we will take a room somewhere. And tomorrow, we can find a place to make our home. Somewhere we can be safe."

Beth smiled. "Somewhere we can be together."

They had been in their new lodgings for a week when there was a knock at the door. Beth looked up from the sketches of the gown she was designing.

"Are you expecting anyone?" her mother asked.

Beth shook her head. She went to the door and opened it a crack, surprised to find Doctor Field on the doorstep. The day she and Caroline had found their new home, she had written to the doctor, telling him all that had transpired. But she had not expected to find him at her door.

"Forgive the intrusion," he said, his cheeks colouring slightly. "I thought to see how you and your mother were doing."

Beth's lips turned up. "My mother and I are doing just fine, Doctor Field. Thank you for your concern." She found herself taking a step closer to him.

Field cleared his throat. He reached into his pocket and pulled out a letter. "This arrived at the asylum this morning. For your mother."

Beth took the letter. It was a stark reminder that their family knew not of Caroline's whereabouts. She had not even dared to tell her brothers and sisters of her freedom, for fear of their father finding out.

"Thank you," said Beth. "I'll see that she gets it."

Field smiled, holding her gaze for a second. He looked down, then back up at her, his cheeks colouring slightly. "There is one other thing, Miss Thursday." He peered at her shyly. "I was wondering if perhaps you might permit me to call on you?" He hesitated. "I understand if you'd rather I didn't. I'm sure the sight of me must evoke some rather unpleasant memories for you. And—"

He stopped speaking as Beth's face broke into a broad smile. "The sight of you is anything but unpleasant," she said, taking his hands. "I will never be anything but happy to see you." She looked into his eyes. "You believed me when no one else did. You risked your livelihood to save me. And you reunited me with my mother. For that, I am endlessly grateful."

Nathan smiled. "I only did what I thought was right."

Impulsively, Beth rose onto her tiptoes and pressed her lips against his. He slid his arms around her, returning her kiss. Beth felt warmth flood her. She held her head against his chest for a moment, listening to the steady thud of his heart.

Too soon, he pulled away. "I will see you again very soon," he said with a shy smile.

Beth grinned. "I look forward to it."

She watched as he disappeared down the stairs. Involuntarily, she brought a hand to her mouth, feeling where his lips had touched hers.

"Was that young Doctor Field?" asked Lady Caroline, appearing behind Beth.

She nodded.

Her mother smiled. "I do believe you are blushing, Beth."

Beth felt the colour in her cheeks intensifying. She held out the letter. "He wanted to bring you this. Someone sent it to the asylum."

Lady Caroline frowned as she took the letter from Beth's hands. She looked down at the circle of red wax. "This is the Derbyshire seal," she said, her voice darkening a little.

Beth's shoulders tensed. "Is it from your father?"

Lady Caroline snapped open the seal and began to read.

"No," she said finally. "It's from my elder brother." She lowered the page. "My father passed away last week. A fever. It took him suddenly…" She faded out, her lips parted with disbelief.

"Oh," said Beth. "Mama, I'm so dreadfully sorry. I…" She wrapped her arms around her mother and held her tightly.

Lady Caroline let out her breath. "It doesn't feel real," she murmured. She peered down at the letter again. "I can't believe it." She kissed Beth on her forehead. "We're going back home. To the family home."

"We are?"

"Yes. It's where we belong. It's where our family is. My brother is not my father by any means." Lady Caroline's face broke into a warm smile. "I've been waiting seventeen years to bring you home, my darling. I'm not going to wait any longer."

EPILOGUE

Nathan Field hunched and scrawled his signature at the bottom of the pages spread out across his desk. He smiled to himself. The documents were the products of months of work, outlining his proposed reforms for the treatment of mental illness here at Bethlem Royal Hospital. If approved by the board, the reforms would make a vast difference to the lives of the current patients. And the lives of countless patients to come. The name Bedlam may no longer be feared.

This was what he had dreamed of when he had started to study illnesses of the mind all those years ago. This was the difference he had hoped to make. He wished his mother was around to see.

He turned down the lamp in his office and made

his way through the building towards the physician's quarters behind the asylum. After Miller's passing, the rooms had been offered to him, and Nathan had been only too happy to accept.

He floated from room to room, smoothing the white tablecloth, checking the coal stores, fluffing the feather pillows on the four-poster bed. Tomorrow, he would be bringing his new wife back here to start their lives together. He wanted everything to be perfect.

"I understand," he'd said to Beth, clutching her hands, "if you'd rather live away from the asylum. We can live anywhere in London you wish."

Beth shook her head. "I want to live here. With you. I want to see you make a difference to this place. I want to watch you help the people who need help. And I want to watch you do it in the way you believe to be right."

BETH FOLLOWED the guard along the dank, grey corridors of the debtors' prison. The guard gestured to a cell at the end of the passage.

Beth nodded. "Let me speak to him first."

The guard nodded.

Beth walked slowly up to the door of the cell. There were three men inside, each huddled in a corner of the room. Their heads were drooped, their hair unruly and their clothes grimy and ragged. One of them was snoring softly.

Beth peered at the man in the far corner. "Mr Whitaker?"

He looked up in surprise. "Elizabeth." He did not sound the way she remembered. His voice was softer, gentler. Kinder? "What are you doing here?" he asked.

Beth smiled. "You're being released, Mr Whitaker."

He climbed to his feet. He showed signs of growing old, Beth realised. His face was riddled with creases, his shoulders beginning to sag. "Released?"

She nodded.

Though Mr Whitaker was not the kindest man Beth had ever known, she had been unable to push him from her mind. After all, he had given her a chance at a new life. He had made mistakes, yes, but Beth knew everyone did. She thought of him often, languishing as he was in the debtors' prison.

She had shared her thoughts with Lady Caroline one night as they sat around the supper table.

"You must release him," her mother had said. "We

have the money now. My brother has seen to it that you and I will never go wanting."

Beth hesitated. "Can I truly take that money from your family?"

"*Our* family," Lady Caroline corrected. She reached across the table and took Beth's hand. "This man gave you a home when I couldn't do so myself. Whatever else he may have done, he doesn't deserve to spend the rest of his life in prison."

Her mother was right, Beth decided. Mr Whitaker had given her a second chance at life. And she would do the same for him.

"Released?" Mr Whitaker said again, his watery grey eyes looking into Beth's. "But how?"

"I'll explain on the way home," she said with a smile, standing back to let the guards unlock the door. Mr Whitaker stood motionless for a moment, staring into the corridor with disbelief. He clutched Beth's fingers with gnarled, papery hands.

"Elizabeth," he said. "Was all this your doing?"

She smiled. "It was my mother's."

* * *

THE NEXT MORNING, Beth stood in her dressing room staring at her reflection in the mirror. She had stitched her wedding dress herself: a simple but elegant cream gown that spilt into a train behind her. It felt strange wearing such an elaborate item of clothing. This was the type of dress she would sew for her wealthy clients. It was not the type of gown she had ever imagined wearing herself.

At first, she had planned to make herself something far more understated to be married in. Perhaps she would even wear her blue woollen dress.

But Lady Caroline would not hear of it. "You are part of a noble family," she had insisted. "And your wedding is a very special occasion." She took Beth's hands and looked her in the eye. "Make yourself a fine gown, my darling. You deserve it."

Beth smoothed the silky folds of her skirts, inhaling deeply to steady her nerves. While she had given in to her mother on the gown, Beth had been adamant that the wedding remain an intimate affair.

"Just family," she said, the word leaving a warmth inside her.

Family...

"Forgive me, Elizabeth," Mr Whitaker had said to her as they rode in the carriage back to the Derbyshire manor the previous night. "I know I put you through some very difficult times. I had a lot of time to think in prison. A lot of time to reflect on my actions." He sighed. "After Emily died, I…"

Beth shook her head. "I know. I struggled when Mrs Whitaker died too. There's no need to apologise. It's in the past."

Mr Whitaker looked down. "It's very good of you to say that, Elizabeth. But—"

Impulsively, Beth clamped a hand over his. "It's in the past," she said again, meeting his eyes. "Please. Let's both move past it."

He gave a nod, giving her a small smile. "I'd like that very much."

"I'm to be married tomorrow," Beth grinned. "And I would very much like it if you could be there. After all, you and Mrs Whitaker were the first family I ever had."

"I ALWAYS SAID you were a wonderful seamstress," her mother said, appearing behind her. Lady Caroline was dressed in the crimson evening gown Beth had sewn for her on one of her early visits to the shop. Beth thought of the countless hours she had spent hunched over her sewing table in the storeroom, determined to create a flawless product for her mysterious new client.

She had known then that Lady Caroline was an important patron. But she could never have anticipated just how important.

She turned to face her mother, her finely stitched skirts swelling around her. "I'm glad you convinced me to make this gown, Mama. I would never have done it on my own."

Lady Caroline smiled and bent to kiss her cheek. "Nathan is going to be beside himself when he sees you."

Beth's nerves gave way to a swell of excitement. She could hardly wait to become Nathan's wife. Could hardly wait for the life that lay ahead.

Lady Caroline held out her hand. "Come now, my darling, we'd best to get to the church. Can't keep your husband to be waiting."

Printed in Great Britain
by Amazon